THE TEXA

All The News You Need To Know...And More!

A mysterious fire on the Montoya ranch seems to be all anyone can talk about these days. Well, that and the fact that Justin Dupree has been seen canoodling with an unnamed woman at the Texas Cattleman's Club. Could this be the same woman the Lone Star playboy has moved into his luxurious penthouse? Because if we had to "name" this woman, we'd be calling her Alicia Montoya...and that would equal a whole passel of trouble.

For, not long ago, we recall a certain Dupree brother accusing a certain Montoya brother of some dirty deeds. Has the hatchet been buried between these families...or is the feud about to go into overdrive when word of the Dupree-Montoya merger (and we mean that, literally) gets out?

Dear Reader,

As you can probably tell from the title of this book, my heroine Alicia Montoya is a virgin. A twenty-six-year-old virgin.

I can already hear the scoffs of disbelief. People seem incredulous that a woman could grow into adulthood without ever experiencing sex. I suspect, however, that there are a lot more adult virgins out there than many people realize.

For Alicia, a strict convent-school upbringing and a protective older brother built a strong moral code and kept her chastity belt firmly locked. Before she knew it, she'd missed that "window of opportunity" in the late teen years, when most of us dip our feet in the waters of sensuality.

It happens. I know people who were in the same situation. Outgoing, fun, friendly women who just never met the right person and suddenly found themselves in their mid-twenties, wondering what went wrong. At that point sexual inexperience can become awkward, an embarrassing and shameful secret.

Luckily for Alicia, she meets just the man to help her explore her sexuality in a nonjudgmental way. Alicia's innocence and sweetness are, in turn, refreshing— and ultimately life changing—for jaded Justin Dupree. I hope you enjoy reading their story as much as I enjoyed writing it.

Jennifer Lewis

JENNIFER LEWIS

THE MAVERICK'S VIRGIN MISTRESS

Silhouette® Desire

Published by Silhouette Books

America's Publisher of Contemporary Romance

Special thanks and acknowledgment to Jennifer Lewis for her contribution to the Texas Cattleman's Club: Maverick County Millionaires miniseries.

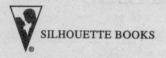

SILHOUETTE BOOKS

ISBN-13: 978-0-373-76977-3

THE MAVERICK'S VIRGIN MISTRESS

Recycling programs
for this product may
not exist in your area.

Visit Silhouette Books at www.eHarlequin.com

Printed in U.S.A.

Books by Jennifer Lewis

Silhouette Desire

The Boss's Demand #1812
Seduced for the Inheritance #1830
Black Sheep Billionaire #1847
Prince of Midtown #1891
*Millionaire's Secret Seduction #1925
*In the Argentine's Bed #1931
*The Heir's Scandalous Affair #1938
The Maverick's Virgin Mistress #1977

*The Hardcastle Progeny

JENNIFER LEWIS

has been dreaming up stories for as long as she can remember and is thrilled to be able to share them with readers. She has lived on both sides of the Atlantic and worked in media and the arts before she grew bold enough to put pen to paper. Happily settled in New York with her family, she would love to hear from readers at jen@jen-lewis.com. Visit her Web site at www.jenlewis.com.

For Anne, Carol, Jerri, Kate, Leeanne and Marie

Texas Cattleman's Club: Maverick County Millionaires

One

Who on earth could be calling at this time of night?

Alicia Montoya reached out from under the covers and groped for the phone on her bedside table. She squinted at the green numerals on the clock.

2:07. *What the heck?*

She lifted the phone to her ear.

"Hello?"

"You're okay. Thank God."

"Who is this?" Her sleepy whisper was barely audible.

"Hi, beautiful."

Oh, boy. His rich, deep voice flowed into her ear and started to awaken parts of her she'd never even known she had until she met Rick Jones. "Hi, Rick."

"I'm so glad you're fine."

Alicia glanced at the clock again. "I was fine until the phone woke me. Didn't I tell you not to call me at home?"

She wondered if her brother Alex had heard the phone. Probably. She was a deep sleeper so it may have been ringing for a while.

Pretty much nothing could happen in the Houston-metro area without her brother being aware of it. Any minute now he'd come barreling in to see what was going on.

"Sweetheart, are you sure you're not married?" Rick teased her relentlessly about her insistence on keeping their relationship secret.

If you could call it a relationship. They hadn't actually kissed yet, but they'd held hands once. That counted, right?

"I'm most definitely not married." She laughed. "Not even close. But I told you my brother is insanely overprotective. Believe me, you do not want him to know you're calling me at two in the morning."

"Why not? You're a grown woman. You can do whatever you want at two in the morning." His tone suggested there were some delicious things they could be doing together at this very moment.

Alicia wriggled under her warm sheets. What would it be like to have Rick right here in bed with her? To run her fingertips over his hard chest or through his silky dark hair?

She had no idea what that would be like, and if Alex learned about Rick, she wouldn't get a chance to find out.

"Trust me on this. It's better if he doesn't know about you. Why are you calling me in the middle of the night, anyway? To torment me with the sound of your sexy voice?"

She smiled in the privacy of darkness. She'd never met a man she felt so comfortable around. With Rick, she could relax enough to tease and flirt. To just…be herself.

"Actually, I was calling to see if you're okay. I'm watching TV and there's breaking coverage of a big fire in Somerset right now. It's hard to tell what's going on in the dark but it almost looks like El Diablo."

"What?" Alicia wondered if she was dreaming. "Our ranch is fine."

Still, fear pricked through her and she slid out of bed onto the cool wood floor. "Hold on, let me look out the window." She hurried across the room and pulled back the thick curtains.

"Oh, my God." Her hand flew to her mouth. An orange glow pierced the darkness.

The flashing lights of emergency vehicles moved along the drive through the ranch, and even through the insulated glass she heard the throb of a helicopter circling overhead.

"It's on fire! The barn! Oh, no, the animals are in there—" She darted across the dark room to the closet.

"I'm coming over."

"No, please don't." Panic flashed through her as she tugged on jeans under her nightshirt. "Whatever's going on, you coming here will make it worse. I have to find Alex. The calves…." She struggled to pull on a pair of boots. "I've got to go."

"Please, let me come."

"No, Rick. Not now. I'll call you as soon as I can." She hung up the phone.

"Alex!" She called out into the hallway of the big ranch house.

A light shone downstairs, and Alex's bedroom door stood open. "Alex, are you here?"

No answer.

She dashed down the stairs two at a time and ran to the front door. She opened it to the smell of smoke and the wail of sirens.

A mass of heaving flame engulfed the barn roof and lit the darkness all the way to the house. "Alex!"

Alicia took off running across the lawn that separated the house from the barn. She could see figures moving, running in the eerie glow from the fire. Shouting mingled with the roar of flames crackling, wood splintering and water gushing from hoses.

"Alex, where are you?" Fear made her voice crack.

Alex was always at the center of everything. She knew with every cell of her body that he was inside that burning barn.

Heart pounding, she raced toward the fire. He might be bossy and overbearing, but he was also the best brother and the warmest, most caring man in the world.

He'd raised her since their parents died and managed to scrape and struggle to provide a good life for them— a wonderful life, now that he was so successful.

A figure rushed up to her in the dark and she recognized one of the ranch hands. "Diego, have you seen Alex?"

"He sent me to wake you. He said to make sure you stay inside the house until he comes."

"He's okay?"

Diego hesitated. "He's trying to rescue the calves."

"Oh, no! I knew he was in there. We have to get him out." She started running to the barn.

Diego grabbed her sleeve. "Miss Alicia, please. Alex wouldn't want you near the fire."

"I don't care what that stubborn fool wants. I've got to get him out of there."

She wrenched her arm free and took off running again. She wasn't the Our Lady of Fatima senior track champion for nothing.

She heard Diego behind her, pleading for her to stop, protesting that Alex had personally entrusted him with her safety and that if he found out—

"There he is!" She saw him emerge from the vast doorway on one side of the barn, driving a herd of calves in front of him.

The young cows were confused and ran in all directions—even trying to get back into the burning barn—as the workers tried to shove them out into the safety of the darkness.

Alicia ran into their midst and grabbed hold of the collar of the calf nearest her. "Come on, princess, you don't want to go back in there." She tugged it away from the doorway.

The hot glow of flame brightened the inside of the barn and seared her skin like noonday sun. Cinders whirled in the smoky air, and ash pricked at her eyes. Every instinct told her to run far, far away.

But she turned to see Alex heading back inside. She gave the calf a slap on the rump to drive it out and plunged for the doorway, toward Alex.

"Alejandro Montoya! You get out of that burning barn or I'll—"

Alex wheeled around. "Alicia, you shouldn't be here. I told Diego—"

"I know what you told Diego, but I'm here now and you need to get out of this barn before the roof collapses. The whole ridgeline is on fire!"

He frowned and glanced back into the barn. "I'll just check to make sure they're all out."

"No!" She grabbed the front of his shirt. His face was almost black with soot but his dark eyes gleamed with purpose.

Desperation made tears spring to her eyes. "Don't risk your life!"

"We've got them all out!" A voice shouted from the darkness. "I counted. All forty-five calves are safe."

"Thank God." Alex grabbed Alicia and threw her over his shoulder in a fireman's lift that knocked the breath from her lungs.

Alicia fought the urge to kick and protest his overbearing reaction. But he was running from the barn, so at least she'd got him heading in the right direction.

"You need to get back in the house and stay there until I come for you!" he shouted as he set her down on her feet a safe distance from the barn.

"I'm not a child, Alex. I can help."

"Nothing's going to help save the barn." Alex winced as a sidewall gave way and the roof started to lean to one side, like a ship keeling over in rough seas.

"It was here before the house. It's over a hundred years old. It's been home and shelter to thousands of animals, and now…" He shook his head.

Alicia bit her lip. She knew how much every inch of this ranch meant to her brother. He'd sweated and saved and worked so hard for it.

Buying El Diablo had been a crowning moment in

both of their lives. The proof that despite all the odds stacked against them, they'd made it and were going to be fine.

She looked back at the barn, now a heaving mass of bright flame. "What happened?"

"We don't know. The fire came out of nowhere. Thank heaven we have smoke alarms that woke Dave and Manny in the apartment above it. They called the fire department, but the building was already going up by the time the first truck arrived."

A tall man strode toward them. Reflected flames illuminated his police badge and the handcuffs glinting at his waist.

"This way, please." He gestured to the driveway where a host of different emergency vehicles winked and flashed their lights in the orange half-light. "We need you all in one place."

"I'm the owner," Alex said. "I need to protect my animals."

The tall policeman squared his shoulders. "Everyone must be interviewed for the investigation."

"What do you mean, investigation?" Alicia squinted through the firelit darkness.

"It's early yet, but the fire marshal thinks this fire was deliberately set. They found empty gas containers near where the blaze started."

Alicia bit her lip. *Who would do this?*

Alex stood up for himself, and as a result he'd made some enemies, but who could hate him—or her—enough to destroy the ranch?

"Arson?" Alex's voice rumbled like a train. "If I find out who did it I'll—"

"Please, sir. Come this way. We have to take a statement from everyone, and I need your cooperation."

Alex blew out a snort of disgust and took Alicia's hand. "Whoever did this will pay."

She kept her mouth shut. No use arguing with him at a time like this. Better to get him out of danger and focus on getting through this awful night.

They picked their way across the grass. An ember landed on Alex's shirt and Alicia slapped it out with her palm.

A strange thought occurred to her. "Didn't Lance Brody's place have a fire recently?"

"There was a blaze at Brody Oil and Gas, yes. That swine had the nerve to accuse *me* of setting it. As if I would stoop to something like that." He clucked his tongue.

She frowned. "If Lance Brody really thinks you burned his building, could he have done this as revenge?"

She could tell by the look on Alex's face that he'd already thought of this. The rivalry between Alex and Lance Brody went back all the way to Maverick High School, where they'd jostled for position on the soccer team. The last thing she needed was to fan the flames of that rivalry.

"I'm sure it wasn't him." She waved her hand in the smoky air. "I don't know why I just said that. Why would a successful businessman get involved in a criminal act?"

"They have paid flunkeys to do their dirty work," Alex growled. "I wouldn't put anything past Lance Brody, or his brother, Mitch. I've been a burr under their saddles for years. Maybe this is their way of trying to push me out of town."

He turned to the barn, where the roof had now collapsed and flames licked out of the hayloft windows.

His eyes flashed with a mix of anger and pain. "But no one's going to run me off El Diablo, and whoever did this will regret the day they were born."

At lunch the next day, Alex paced back and forth across the dining room at the ranch, his burger growing cold on the plate.

"Alicia, it's not safe for you here right now. If someone's out to get me, who knows what they'll try next. You can stay with El Gato."

Alicia looked up from her plate as goose bumps spread over her skin. "I'll be fine here. Besides, you need someone to look after you."

She pointed to his plate with her best schoolmarm expression. "Eat your food."

"I'm serious, 'Manita. It's not safe."

"Staying with Paul 'El Gato' Rodriquez is what's not safe. I know you won't hear a word against him, but everyone knows he's involved in drug trafficking."

Alex grunted as he slid into his chair. "They just don't like to see a Latino make a lot of money. You'd be shocked if you knew how many people think I'm involved with drugs or guns or something. They don't think we can make money the old-fashioned way like they do."

He took a bite of his hamburger. "That's why joining the Texas Cattleman's Club was such a big deal for me. When I'm there, I'm one of them, a member of the club. They have to smile at me and act polite, even if they'd really prefer to see me hang." He grinned. "I love that."

Alicia hated the way her brother still felt like an outsider, even now that he was one of the richest men in the area.

"You were accepted into the Texas Cattleman's Club because you're a man of honor and an upstanding member of Somerset society. You *are* one of them."

"That's one of the many reasons why I love you, sis. You have such great faith in the human spirit." He winked as he took a sip of soda. "But you're still not staying here. El Gato can protect you from anything."

"I'm sure he can. He's probably got nine millimeters stashed in the trunk of his car, but frankly that kind of 'protection' makes me nervous."

"He's one of us. When the going gets tough, sometimes it's better to stick with your own."

"I don't consider a suspected criminal to be one of 'my own' in any way."

"You know what I mean. When you come from the barrio, you see the world a little differently."

"You're talking as if I didn't grow up in the same house as you." Alicia bristled. She hated when her brother treated her like a kid. "I was there, too, remember? I know what hard times are like, and I'm more than glad to have left them behind. You need to get rid of that chip on your shoulder," she said, still trying to figure out how to change Alex's mind. "I could go stay with one of the neighbors."

Alex narrowed his eyes. "I don't trust those people. Not right now."

"How about Maria Nunez? You've known her as long as I have. You let me sleep over at her house when we were in school. I'm sure she won't mind me staying a few nights."

He grunted. "I always suspected that Maria of having a wild streak. Still, her parents are good people. Does she live at home?"

Alicia laughed. "No. She's twenty-six years old, remember? She has an apartment in Bellaire. Very safe area."

"If she's not married, she should be at home with her family." Alex took a swig of coffee.

"It's not the nineteenth century anymore, Alex. Deal with it. I'll call her right away. If she says no, then I'll go to El Gato, okay?"

The lie tingled on her tongue for a second, since she had no intention of going anywhere near Paul Rodriquez and his crew of scary henchmen, even if he was Alex's oldest friend.

Alex clucked with disapproval. "Stubborn."

"Sensible." She smiled sweetly. "You know I am. Don't you trust me?"

Her heart fluttered as she realized he had every reason not to.

"All right, you can stay with Maria. You are sensible, and I'm very proud of you. I love you like crazy, 'Manita, you know that?"

"I do, and I love you, too, you big bear of a brother." She rounded the table and gave him a kiss on his thick head of hair before going upstairs, heart pounding.

Alicia closed her bedroom door carefully before picking up her phone.

She hadn't even dared add Rick's number to her favorites, in case Alex happened to pick up her phone and notice a new number there among her old friends from school.

Anticipation mingled with anxiety made her fingers twitchy as she dialed.

It rang only once.

"Hey, beautiful." That soft, seductive voice.

A smile spread over her face. "What if I'm not looking at all beautiful right now?"

"Impossible. You can't help it," he said, making her feel warm all over. "I saw on the news they put the fire out and that no one was hurt. What a relief."

"Tell me about it. We rescued every single calf, only a few scrapes and cuts on them. The barn is gone, though. Nothing left but soggy blackened wood. And there was a six-month supply of good hay in there that we'd put up for the winter."

"I'm sorry to hear that. I hope it was insured."

"It was, but the barn is irreplaceable. It was one of the first buildings in Somerset. A true historic landmark. I was hoping to get it preservation status, but I guess I can forget about that now." She sighed. "It could have been much worse. If the wind was blowing harder, the house could have caught fire."

"I wish I were there to give you a hug."

"Trust me, I could really use one."

"Then since you won't let me set foot on El Diablo, you're going to have to come here to get one."

Adrenaline flashed through Alicia. How could she ask this delicately? Or even indelicately? "Can I spend the night with you?"

A beat of silence made her pulse throb, but it was followed by a rushed, "Of course." His enthusiasm almost made her laugh.

"Wow, that sounded bad, didn't it? It's just that Alex

doesn't think it's safe for me to stay here. The police think the fire was set deliberately and he's worried the arsonist will come back to finish the job. He wants me to go stay with an old school friend of his, but I don't like the guy."

"I don't want you near any guy except me. And in case you didn't know, my suite at the Omni has four bedrooms."

"You're kidding."

"Not even a little. Pack your bags and come on over."

"My car was parked behind the barn. It pretty much melted."

"No sweat, I'll come get you." She could almost hear him panting like an excited puppy.

She smiled. "I don't think so. If Alex sees your car, it'll ruin everything. I'll ask him to drive me to the Texas Cattleman's Club. That way he won't suspect anything and you can pick me up there. I could be there by four this afternoon."

"I'll meet you outside."

Alicia frowned. It might be nice to hang out at the club a while. She wouldn't mind showing her new beau off to her friends. But maybe he'd just want to get her bags back to his place.

Or get *her* back to his place.

A naughty smile snuck across her lips and her body tingled with anticipation. She'd be all alone with Rick in his hotel suite, and she had a feeling that tonight would be a night she'd never forget.

"Great, I'll meet you by the front door. See you then."

She hung up the phone, downright jumpy with excitement.

She'd recently bought some sexy lingerie at Sweet Nothings in anticipation of becoming more intimate with Rick. She had it hidden away in the back of her dresser drawer so Alex wouldn't stumble across it while looking for something.

Now hopefully she'd finally get a chance to put it on—and watch Rick take it off.

Justin pressed the button to raise the roof on his Porsche convertible. He wasn't sure Alicia would appreciate the wind in her hair.

Like every inch of her that he'd had the pleasure to see so far, her dark hair was silky smooth and perfectly groomed.

And he was looking forward to seeing a lot more of her now that he'd have her all to himself, in his suite, for days—and nights—on end.

He'd like to see desire flare in those big brown eyes, and run his eager hands all over her glowing olive skin.

A wicked grin spread across his face.

Then he wiped if off.

Cool your jets. First of all, Alicia was traumatized by the fire at the ranch she shared with her brother. She needed his support, not his hands pawing all over her.

Second, she had no idea who he really was.

He cursed and tapped his fingers impatiently on the wheel as he waited at a traffic light.

Why did he have to call himself Rick Jones when he met her?

Sure, he used the name often, but usually for making hotel reservations or when he met someone who had "gold digger" written all over her. There were definitely times when being Justin Dupree—of *those* Duprees—was a serious liability.

Once people knew he had more money than God, they treated him differently. And he was tired of the society press tailing him like a bloodhound, looking for more stories for their gossip columns. Thanks to them, he now had an embarrassing reputation as a playboy that was really only half-deserved.

Okay, maybe three-quarters. But that was all in the past.

He was thirty now and more settled. He wasn't so excited about partying all night. Lately, he wanted to spend quality time getting to know a woman before he slept with her.

Take Alicia. How many dates had they been on? Maybe eight, and he still hadn't slept with her.

Or even kissed her.

He blew out a breath. The light turned green and he honked his horn to get the car in front of him moving. Eight dates and not even a kiss on the lips? That was ridiculous. And he wasn't entirely sure how it had happened, either.

There was something so perfect about Alicia, so pure and sweet and gentle, that he never quite felt right about asking her back to his place. She was the kind of girl you'd send flowers to, the kind whose parents you'd chat with when you picked her up at her house. The kind you'd buy a corsage for on prom night.

Except that they were both adults and her parents had been dead for years. Why did Alicia Montoya turn him from a hardened ladies' man back into an eager and apprehensive schoolboy?

He wove through traffic on the beltway and took the exit for Somerset. Alicia Montoya was something else, and he didn't mind waiting for the chance to weave his fingers into her soft hair.

"I'm not Rick Jones." How hard was it to just say it?

One snag was that Alex knew him. He'd used the alias partly so he could ask Alicia about Alex and maybe dig up some useful information about him for Mitch and Lance Brody. If he actually did go to El Diablo, Alex would recognize him from the club.

And then there was Alicia herself.

Usually once he told a girl he was actually Justin Dupree, she laughed off the deception and fawned all over him, thrilled to be dating the notorious shipping heir instead of some regular guy.

Alicia though…

He let out a low whistle. He suspected she wouldn't take the deception lightly. She'd gone to a convent school, for crying out loud. She carried white linen handkerchiefs in her purse. Her French-tipped finger-nails did not look like they'd ever been anywhere Mother Superior wouldn't approve of.

Did he really want to blow his chance of feeling those luscious, manicured nails rake down his back?

No. He didn't. Which was why he wasn't going to mention the little name issue just yet. He'd wait until the drama of the fire blew over. Until he'd held her in his arms and whispered sweet nothings in her ear.

Until he'd made hot, wild love to her all night long.

Then he'd tell her.

Two

Alicia paced under the elegant awning outside the Texas Cattleman's Club.

Bees buzzed around flowers blooming in the carved-stone planters. Sunlight glistened on the polished-marble walkway and flashed off the brass accents on the door as members came and went, waving hello and stopping to commiserate about the fire.

Alicia tried to act normal, as though she wasn't about to embark on possibly the biggest "first" in her life.

She'd never spent the night at a man's house before.

She'd never...

She'd never done a lot of things, and she hoped to rectify that, starting tonight.

The hushed sound of a powerful engine made her glance up. Rick pulled up in front of the awning and leaned out of the driver's seat of his silver Porsche.

The sun shone in his tousled dark hair. "How do you manage to look more gorgeous every time I see you?" He cocked his head and fixed his bold blue eyes on hers.

Alicia blushed. She had gone to a little extra effort with her appearance today. She wanted everything to be perfect.

She gestured to her luggage. "I tried not to pack too much stuff. Just some clothes for work and a few casual things."

Like the pretty lingerie she'd bought last week.

He stowed her bags in the trunk. Black tailored slacks clung to his powerful thighs and a well-cut polo shirt emphasized the width of his shoulders. Was it fair for a man to be so dangerously handsome?

She could hardly believe he was interested in her.

"Do you want to go in?" She gestured to the front door. Cara was inside and she'd love to see the look on her friend's face when she got an eyeful of Rick.

Although she'd met him at the club, she wasn't sure if he was a member. The couple of times she'd mentioned his name to friends, she'd drawn blank stares.

He hesitated and glanced at the double doors that led into the wood-paneled sanctuary. "I'd actually rather get back to the hotel. I have a business call coming. Nothing major, it won't take long."

"Oh, no problem. Let's go then." She tried not to let her disappointment show.

Of course he had business to conduct. She wasn't exactly sure what he did, but judging from the car he drove and the fact that he had a four-bedroom suite at the Houston Omni, it must be pretty darn important.

She couldn't expect him to put his whole life on hold because she needed a place to stay.

At the Omni, the bellhop removed Alicia's bags from the trunk and she felt strangely weightless as she watched them disappear across the glistening marble floor of the lobby.

No turning back now.

Not that she wanted to. Rick was so thoughtful and sweet. He squeezed her hand as they walked to the bank of elevators.

She squeezed back, trying not to let her nerves show. He had no idea this was new for her. That she'd never spent the night with a man before.

Or, in fact, ever had sex.

At age twenty-six.

How shocked would he be if he knew? At this point, it was such a humiliating secret, she even kept it from her girlfriends. Only Maria—who she'd stayed close to since high school—knew the terrible truth.

When Alicia had asked permission to use her as an alibi for her stay at Rick's, Maria had been so excited she could barely get words out. "Who is he?" she asked. "Is he cute? I'll only lie for you if you promise to go all the way!"

Alicia had laughed off Maria's exhortations, but being a virgin at twenty-six was no laughing matter.

She flashed Rick a smile as he pressed the elevator button.

She wasn't even quite sure how it had happened. One minute she was a teenager telling boys she wasn't that kind of girl, the next she was looking in the mirror wondering where her so-called youth went.

Now she'd found the right man to finally initiate her into womanhood. Rick was perfect. Almost too perfect, in fact. She knew Alex would be suspicious of him.

But then Alex was suspicious of everyone.

"Be it ever so humble…" Rick winked as he slid the keycard into the lock.

"Oh, my." Alicia's jaw dropped as the door opened to an elegant interior, lush with fine fabrics and gleaming antiques. "This is a hotel room?"

"Not really. It's more of a furnished apartment with all the amenities. Not too many apartment buildings come with room service, and with all the traveling I do, it's nice to have everything taken care of."

"I guess if you don't have a wife to take care of you, a hotel staff is the next best thing." She smiled, looking around the luxurious environment.

Rick's silence made her turn.

Alicia bit her lip. A wife? What on earth was she thinking? Now he'd suspect her of auditioning for the role.

"And I guess you don't have to worry about mowing your lawn." She tried to push the conversation forward, to distract from her gaffe. "But you probably wouldn't anyway."

Duh! Rick Jones had probably never mowed a lawn in his life. Men who hung out at the Texas Cattleman's Club had "people" for that.

She and Alex were probably the only members who weren't born with silver spoons in their mouths. Another reminder that she was out of her element here in Rick's luxurious penthouse.

"Which bedroom would you like? We're on the

corner so each one gives you a different view of the city."

He ushered her into a large room with gold draperies, an elegant sleigh bed and a panoramic view west over the Galleria area.

"Gee, I don't know if this is fancy enough for me." Alicia grinned.

"I see what you mean. And really, the morning light is better from the east."

He guided her out the door. Pleasure shivered through her at the feel of his hand at the base of her spine.

They entered a room with a large four-poster bed laden with embroidered pillows. Elegant white draperies fluttered slightly in the air-conditioner breeze. The view across the treetops of Memorial Park—all the way to the shimmering skyscrapers of downtown Houston—was breathtaking.

"Then again, sometimes it's annoying being woken up too early."

Gentle pressure from his palm sent heat snaking through her belly. She allowed him to ease her out the door.

The third bedroom had a Japanese flavor with willow-green draperies and images of cranes and lilies on the wall.

The bedpost and furniture were crafted from elegant bamboo. A bubbling fountain ornamented one corner of the bright space.

The view looked down on a wooded bend in the river—a strangely wild vista for this part of the world—and added to the impression of a lush retreat.

Alicia smiled. "Pretty! I like this one."

"Make yourself at home. You can stay as long as you want. And I mean that quite literally. I have the suite reserved for the next two years."

She laughed. How much money did this guy have? This suite probably cost ten thousand dollars a night. "Hopefully, my brother will let me come back home before then, but I appreciate the offer."

Rick's striking blue eyes fixed on hers. "Now, dinner. I usually have it sent up from the hotel restaurant, but we could go out if you prefer."

"I don't want to put you to any trouble."

"If you insisted on me cooking it myself, I think we'd both be in trouble, but as long as professionals are involved, it's no trouble at all." A naughty dimple appeared in his left cheek. "Let me get you a menu."

He slipped out of the room, leaving Alicia to catch her breath.

Her heart pounded under her pale-blue blouse and her high heels sank into the soft carpet.

Houston lay at her feet like a rug unfurled, the sun setting over the trees and rooftops casting a soft glow over the delicate furnishings of the lovely bedroom.

Tonight was the night. By tomorrow morning she'd be a woman in every sense of the word.

Rick appeared in the door with the menu, startling her out of her thoughts. "If you don't like anything on the menu, we can talk to the chef. He's a pretty cool guy. He knows I'm wild about lobster so he saves the best ones for me."

"I love lobster." Alicia looked up. "I always feel guilty eating something that can live so long, but they're too delicious."

"Done." Rick snatched the menu from her fingertips, which tingled as his hand brushed against them. "And your visit here definitely calls for champagne."

They ate in the suite's formal dining room. Champagne sparkled in crystal flutes as candlelight illuminated the details in the wood-paneled walls, and cast shadows across the white, linen tablecloth.

The chef had prepared them an array of different sauces for the lobster and some creative and colorful salads.

The champagne tickled her nose and she was careful to take only the tiniest of sips so she wouldn't get tipsy. She didn't want to miss a single minute of tonight.

Rick leaned forward. "Does Alex have any suspects for the fire?"

Guilt speared Alicia as she realized she'd totally forgotten about Alex and the fire. "I don't think so, but there was a suspicious fire at the Brody headquarters a while back and they had the nerve to blame Alex, so being a guy, he's decided the Brodys might be responsible."

For a moment, she thought she saw a shadow flit across Rick's face. He picked up his glass and took a sip. "I'd think you'd be friends with the Brodys. They're members of the Cattleman's Club."

"Yes, but Alex and Lance have this dumb rivalry dating back to high school. I'm glad it's not medieval times or they'd be challenging each other to jousts. Typical macho silliness."

"So, you don't believe Lance Brody set the fire?" His expression was strangely serious.

"Of course not. Why would a successful businessman want to burn down our barn? That doesn't make any sense at all."

She hesitated. "Alex does have some enemies, though. No one who'd really want to hurt him, but he's trodden on a few toes over the years."

"Haven't we all? It's part of being successful."

She sighed and nodded. "And he rose so far so fast, it put some people's noses out of joint. Did you know Alex used to be the groundskeeper at the club?"

"You're kidding me." His look of genuine shock made her wonder if she shouldn't have told him.

Did Alex want people reminded of his humble beginnings?

"Not for long. Just during part of high school and college. He used to mow the lawns after class. Once his import-export business took off, he quit and he's never looked back."

"I had no idea." Rick raised a brow. "Alex sounds like quite a character."

"He's an amazing man."

"And I guess he doesn't think any guy is good enough for his baby sister." A smile lifted one side of his mouth. "Is that why you won't let me near the house?"

Alicia laughed. "He's overprotective. It drives me nuts. I know he's only like that because he cares about me, but come on—I'm twenty-six!"

He leveled a serious blue gaze at her. "Maybe you should get your own place."

"Oh, I've thought about it, but as far as Alex is concerned, a girl doesn't leave home until she goes to live with her husband."

She blanched. Once again she'd managed to raise the specter of marriage. That spooked most guys right out of the room. "It's a Mexican thing. We're very traditional. You learn to work around it."

At least some people did. Maria had lived on her own for three years.

Maybe I'm just the lamest wimp on earth.

She fished inside her lobster claw, hoping he'd change the subject.

Was he crazy to want an affair with Alicia? Alex Montoya was not someone to tangle with.

Lord knew he put enough distance between himself and his own interfering relatives. Did he really want to get involved with a woman whose brother hovered over her like a shadow?

Justin watched her probe into the red depths of her lobster claw like a surgeon with a scalpel.

She looked up. "What?"

"I've never seen someone eat a lobster with such meticulous precision."

"I like to enjoy every delicious morsel." She smiled and popped a tender piece into her mouth. Like everything else in Alicia's world, her plate was perfectly ordered, not a lettuce leaf out of place.

"You're very detail-oriented."

"I'm a museum curator. We're probably the most detail-oriented people on earth. Except maybe for mailservice workers. But at least we don't have to worry about going postal."

She shot him an infectious grin, then returned to surgery on her lobster.

"I didn't know you were a curator. You must be very accomplished to hold that position at your age."

He'd been impressed and intrigued when she told him she worked at the museum, but for some reason he'd assumed she gave tours or taught classes there. It didn't occur to him she was running the show.

"Oh, I wouldn't say that." A delicate blush darkened her cheeks. "I'm just passionate about my work. The Somerset Museum of Natural History was just getting started when I joined as an archivist. The original curator left for a job at the Smithsonian, and I kind of stepped into the role."

"I'm ashamed to admit I've never been to the museum. What kinds of artifacts do you have?"

"It's an interesting mix. Most of it came from a huge private collection started almost a century ago. Dinosaur bones, fossils, meteorites, that kind of thing. We have some Native American artifacts from a different private collection. My focus has been on objects unique to the Houston area, and in particular to Somerset. This region has some interesting history. People seem to forget that when they talk about knocking down old buildings to put up a strip mall."

Justin's ears pricked up. "You mean the redevelopment of downtown Somerset?"

"Exactly." Alicia tossed her head, which made her thick dark hair swing over her shoulders, golden highlights sparkling in the candlelight. "That would be a travesty."

Interesting. He'd heard rumors that Alex had blocked the redevelopment of a key area that could have meant a big windfall to a couple of club members, including Kevin Novak. "Wouldn't redevelopment be good for the local economy?"

"That's what some people say, but our downtown area is one of the most well-preserved main streets in Texas. The architectural style is unique. Come on, have you ever seen corbelling like the fascia of the old town hall?"

Justin laughed, impressed by her command of architecture. "I can honestly say I haven't." Longhorn cattle with brass horns jutted out beneath the metal roof of the grand old building—Texas-style gargoyles. "I admit the aspirations of the town's founders were writ large in those buildings. It does have its own charm."

Alicia nodded, passion shining in her dark eyes. "And that would all be lost if they were bulldozed to make way for more generic big-box stores. It's like the stuff I see in my job. Once upon a time, that fossil was just another boring insect or fish or leaf. Now it's the only one of its kind that's survived to the present day. A unique glimpse into another time that enriches our understanding of the world around us and its history."

"I've never heard that perspective before." He frowned. "I suspect most people would rather have a dry cleaner closer to home or a Mega Mart where they can get cheap groceries."

"I'm not saying those things aren't important, but downtown Somerset is too special to let it be lost forever. There are plenty of bland, ugly buildings that can be torn down instead." She flashed a wicked grin. "I'd be happy to give them some suggestions."

"Maybe you should."

Justin frowned. He was getting a very different impression of the Montoya family than the one he'd formed based on idle gossip.

He'd assumed her brother stood up to block the redevelopment because he had his own profit-making agenda for the area. Now it almost seemed like he'd stalled the new development to make his history-buff sister happy.

This was not the fearsome and dangerous Alex Montoya of local legend.

Justin sipped his wine and peered at Alicia through narrowed eyes. "What would you do with the downtown?"

"I'd love to see it become a tourist attraction. Some of the buildings are ideal for upscale retail, or for quaint bed-and-breakfast accommodation. I don't think many people in the Houston area have any idea how beautiful Somerset is. It could become popular as a weekend getaway, and that would bring business and tax revenue to the town without destroying its unique charm."

"I'd hire you to do that in a heartbeat."

"Shame you can't." Her luscious lips turned into a smile that heated his blood. "Or can you?" Her brows lifted. "You haven't told me what you do."

Oh, I'm just heir to the largest shipping operation in the western hemisphere.

He wasn't at all sure how she'd react. But if he told her, he'd also have to confess that he was Justin Dupree, not Rick Jones.

"Nothing very interesting. Pushing papers around."

She cocked her head, which made her earrings sparkle in the candlelight. "Didn't you have an important phone call to make?"

"A phone call?"

"At the club, you said you couldn't stay because you had a phone call?"

"Oh, yes."

His little white lie to explain why he couldn't go inside. Once you started with this stuff it was hard to stop.

Still, he didn't want anyone to greet him with a hearty "Hey, Justin" until he'd had a chance to dig himself out of this hole he'd gotten into.

"I forgot about that call. But no matter. The world will continue to turn on its axis."

"I'm sorry to be a distraction. I don't want to get you into trouble."

Her look of concern touched something inside him.

"You are the best distraction I've ever encountered and I'd face all kinds of trouble to spend an evening with you. Tell me more about the natural history of Somerset. Were there dinosaurs around here?"

The sparkle in her eyes made him lean forward so he could enjoy their glow. "Absolutely."

Alicia was sure Rick's eyes would glaze over when she told him about the dig she'd helped out on last summer. Instead, his interest seemed to deepen with each detail she revealed.

Those intense blue irises stayed fixed on hers as she described each bone they unearthed, and how they had preserved and stored them for reassembly at the museum.

If she wasn't mistaken he seemed…fascinated.

The candlelight flickered over the hard planes of his handsome face while he asked intriguing questions and actually *listened* to her answers.

Which only increased the turmoil of excitement in her stomach. How could anyone be this wonderful?

He'd said he pushed papers for a living, but his tan suggested time spent outdoors and the athletic cut of his body belonged to a man of action. There was clearly more to discover about Rick Jones.

But everything she'd learned so far had her dangerously close to falling in love with the man.

Her dessert fork clinked against her glass as she set it down too hard.

They'd known each other less than three weeks. She had no intention of actually falling in love with him or anyone else. But you didn't have to be in love to kiss.

Her mouth twitched at the prospect of pressing her lips to his. His mouth was wide, mobile, with a way of lifting slightly higher on one side than the other like he had a naughty secret.

"I have a secret." His words took her by surprise, as if he'd spoken her thoughts aloud.

"You do?" Her pulse quickened.

"I had something made for you." His blue eyes twinkled.

Alicia stared at him. "What?" She hoped it wasn't freaky lingerie with slits in strange places. Maybe now she'd discover the dark side of Rick Jones. There had to be something horribly wrong with him, didn't there?

Rick reached into his pocket, which really set her heart pounding.

Of course it's not a ring, you idiot. He barely knows you. Stop watching so many old movies.

He pulled out a jewelry box.

He laughed at her expression. "Don't panic. It doesn't bite." That wicked dimple deepened as he handed her the box over the remains of their pecan pie.

Alicia took it with shaking fingers and tried not to look like he'd just given her a stick of dynamite. She flipped the lid.

A single blue gem attached to a fine silver chain sparkled against white velvet. A bold five-pointed star shone through the glittering facets.

"Texas topaz! Oh, my goodness, it's lovely."

The sparkly stone was almost the same haunting blue as Rick's eyes.

"I found the stone years ago on a trip into the Texas Hill country. The rock-hound friend I was with couldn't believe I found a gem like this on my first try. I never knew what to do with it."

He glanced down at the box in her hand. "When you told me you worked at the natural history museum, I knew I'd been saving it for you. I had it cut at a place downtown."

"Julie's Gems? Julie's been my biggest supporter in saving the historic buildings."

"That's the place." He grinned. "And I noticed you wear blue a lot. It kind of matches the dress you have on."

Alicia tried not to melt into a puddle on the floor. "You are without a doubt the most thoughtful and generous man I've ever met." She couldn't keep emotion out of her voice. "It's beautiful. Let me try it on."

"I'll help you." He rose and rounded the table.

Alicia stood, smoothing out the skirt of the simple silk dress she'd changed into for dinner.

She did wear blue almost every day. It had always been her favorite color.

She lifted the single flawless gem out of its box and dangled it on the pretty chain. Pleasure and anticipation tingled through her as Rick moved behind her.

His spicy and intriguing scent wrapped around her, and she could feel the heat of his skin through their clothes. His fingertips brushed hers as he took the delicate necklace, and Alicia suppressed a shiver of delight.

He lifted the delicate chain around her neck and fastened the clasp.

"Let me see." With a deft movement of his hands he spun her gently toward him. Their eyes met and a flash of something passed between them.

Pure lust, probably.

Not being experienced, Alicia couldn't put a name to any of the sensations pouring through her.

Only inches separated her from Rick and as they stood facing each other, the space between them seemed to crackle with energy.

Rick held her gaze. "Magnificent." His eyes rested not on the finely cut gem, but directly on hers, as if the compliment was intended for her rather than the jewel.

Alicia's lips parted, but no words came out. Instead, she stared at Rick's lips, issuing a silent invitation for them to join hers.

Their mouths met in an instant, lips crushing together as their arms slid around each other. Alicia heard a slight moan issue from her mouth as the warm, firm pressure of Rick's kiss sent a wave of pleasure rippling to her toes.

Their tongues touched, tentative and gentle, asking a sensual question.

Rick's broad hands closed around her waist, firm and steady. Her fingers reached up into his silky dark hair as their kiss deepened. Her breasts crushed against his chest, nipples hard with desire as he pulled her tighter into his embrace.

His thin polo shirt separated her from the taut muscle of his chest and suddenly she longed to strip off the layers of clothing between them. To feel his skin against hers.

Rick pulled his lips away slowly. The sensation hurt. She'd longed for this kiss and waited and hoped.... And now it was over. But the ache of longing hadn't diminished. It throbbed—stronger—deep inside her.

Alicia drew in a sharp breath. "Thank you."

"For the kiss?" Rick tilted his head, bemused.

"For the necklace." Heat rose up her neck. "But the kiss was lovely, too."

And hopefully, just the beginning. Would he invite her into his room to spend the night? She hoped so, but how could she make that clear without being forward?

She'd spent so much time trying to keep boys' hands away from anything below her neck that she had no idea how to encourage Rick in that direction now that she was ready.

"It's late," Rick murmured.

"Yes." Hope flared in her heart.

They stood, arms entwined, lips inches apart. In her high heels she was almost his height, and if she dared she could reach up and kiss him again right now.

"I think we should go to bed." Rick's eyes glittered like sapphires.

"Oh, yes," breathed Alicia. "I agree." Her belly contracted with excitement.

"Let me show you to your room."

She tried to keep a goofy grin off her face as they

walked across the candlelit living room and into the hallway that led to her room.

Rick's hand at her waist guided her gently, sending awareness trickling along her nerves. The rough silk of her dress chafed against her nipples even through the expensive bra she'd worn.

Tonight's the night.

Alicia tried to keep her breathing steady as he opened the door and ushered her inside.

She'd left the room spotless and perfectly organized—just in case. No makeup scattered on the dressing table or pantyhose spread over the chairs. She'd even turned the sheets back and opened a sachet of lavender into a little dish to add a fresh, floral scent.

She shuddered slightly as Rick pulled her closer and pressed his lips to hers. She rubbed against him, startled and thrilled by the hard length in his pants. Heat flooded her limbs and she wondered if it would be indecent to start unbuckling his belt while she still had control of her fingers.

But he pulled back and rubbed her cheek with his thumb. "Sleep tight, my beauty. I'll see you in the morning."

As the door closed behind him, Alicia fought the urge to scream with frustration.

What's wrong with me?

Three

Justin leaned back against the closed door of his bedroom and cursed the lust that roared through his body like fire. He was hard as any rock in the Texas hills. His muscles ached and throbbed with the urge to pull Alicia closer. To undress her and lick every inch of her warm, silky body. To make her cry out in hunger and desire as he pleasured her all night long.

A low groan escaped his mouth and echoed in the still air of his bedroom.

Thank heaven he'd still managed to behave like a gentleman.

Alicia came to him looking for sanctuary, not seduction. She was shaken by the fire and by the strange accusations of arson flying through the rarefied air of Somerset. It was his duty to comfort her and make her feel safe.

He shook his head as if that might dislodge the

lustful thoughts rambling around his brain. It wasn't her fault she was built like a sex goddess, with curves that could bring a grown man to his knees.

He marched across his room and flipped on the jets in the shower.

Cold.

The sound of her own cry woke Alicia with a start.

She sat upright in bed and searched for the familiar digital face of her clock.

Instead, the stiff tick-tock of an antique carriage clock reminded her that she wasn't at home. In the darkness she had no idea what time the strange clock read.

Sweat pricked her brow and images from her nightmare crowded her mind. The embroidered bedcover clung to her like the rich lace of the dress she'd been wearing in her dream.

A wedding dress.

Standing at a kind of altar—or was it outdoors?—she watched as handsome men in suits and evening dress approached, bearing gifts and smiling.

Some of them looked familiar, like Remy, the exchange student from France she'd dated (very) briefly her sophomore year of college. And Lars, the boy from Minnesota who'd made the mistake of challenging Alex to a game of tennis when he came to pick her up.

Others looked new, unfamiliar, each handsome and smiling and staring at her with the heat of passion in his eyes.

Until a fierce growl erupted out of the night—wait, wasn't it day?—and sent each suitor scurrying into the distance, passion forgotten.

Stop! The silent words had scratched at her throat. *Wait! Don't leave me here all alone.*

Please?

A sob rose in her throat and tears behind her eyelids. The growl filled the air around her again, and she turned, frightened of the monster who'd chased away so many strong men.

But the monster was also a man. Tall and broadly built, his dark eyes filled with…love.

Her brother, Alex.

"Oh, Alex, why do you have to be so suffocating? Let me be. Let me live!" The words rattled in her brain as the first tears flowed.

She realized she'd woken up at the exact moment in the dream when she'd looked down at her hands. They'd been gnarled and spotted with age. Wrinkled and ringless. The hands of an old woman.

She glanced at them now in the dark, relieved by their smooth, familiar outline in the reflected glow of moonlight through the crack in the curtains.

In the dream they'd been different.

She startled awake as the horrible truth of the dream sank in: she was still a virgin. An eighty-year-old virgin.

A racking sob heaved her chest. *Why me?* What was so wrong with her? Sure, she wasn't the most beautiful woman in the world, but ordinary women managed to marry and have children. Or go on dates.

Or even go all the way.

Just once!

She'd been so sure she'd break her losing streak tonight, that Rick would finally pop the rather wizened cherry she'd been keeping secret for years now because it was so horribly embarrassing to be still a virgin.

Twenty-six, for crying out loud! She was probably the only twenty-six-year-old virgin in the entire state of Texas. Or the whole United States.

Maybe even the whole world.

A wail escaped her lips as she collapsed back on to her pillow. At that moment, light streamed into the room as the door was flung open. Rick stood in the doorway.

"Alicia, what's the matter?" His voice rang with concern.

"I…I…I…" *I want to make love to you.*

Did she want him to know that she was a freak? A grown woman who'd never been kissed below the neck? Who'd never seen a man naked, or felt his hands on her bare skin?

Tears streamed down her face.

Rick approached the bed. "Don't cry, Alicia. I know last night was a horrible shock. But at least no one was hurt. They'll rebuild the barn and they'll catch the criminal who set the fire."

Through her fog of tears she felt his fingers caress her tangled hair. But she didn't want comfort. She wanted breathless passion.

She thrust out her arms and wrapped them around his neck, then crushed her mouth against his. Parted in surprise, his lips hesitated a moment before joining in the kiss.

Rising to her knees, she pressed her body against his through her long nightgown. Her nipples hardened against the bare muscle of his chest. The stubble of his cheek was a sweet balm to her fevered skin.

Don't stop! She tightened her grip around him, determined not to let him escape.

"Alicia." He managed to free his mouth for a second to gasp her name. "I'm not sure this…"

She fumbled with the strings of his pajama pants, unsure how her hands had found them, but intent on getting them undone immediately.

"Sweetheart, it's okay." Rick flinched as her hand brushed against his rock-hard erection.

She yanked on a string, but the knot was tight and she couldn't work it loose. Still jerking at it with one hand, she raised the other to tug down the shoulder strap of her nightgown.

The thin satin tore easily and she pulled down the gown to bare her breast. Cool night air tightened her nipple.

"Touch me," she pleaded, still tugging at his pajamas.

Rick lifted a tentative palm to her bare breast. She shuddered hard as he brushed her nipple.

"Alicia, I don't know if this is a good idea." She heard him swallow. "You seem a little…overwrought."

With a burst of elation she pulled open the knot holding his pajamas closed and started to push them down over his hips.

"Really, I think we should slow down." His pulsing erection and husky voice contradicted his words. "How about…a cup of tea?" he croaked.

Alicia froze. "Tea? What is it about me that makes you think of *tea* at a moment like this?" Suddenly, fierce sobs racked her body. "What's wrong with me? What's *wrong?*"

Her words rang out into the silent air of the hotel room and bounced back at her off the polished surfaces.

"Nothing's wrong, Alicia. You've just had a long day and you need some sleep."

"Sleep is the last thing I need." Her voice quavered as she readied herself to make her terrible confession.

Rick's eyes were midnight-blue in the scant light that streamed through the half-open doorway and outlined the ripped muscle of his neck and shoulders.

"I need *you*." Alicia drew in a shuddering breath. "I'm a virgin."

Justin almost fell off the bed. "You're kidding me."

"Would I kid about something like this?" Alicia's big brown eyes glittered with tears.

"Wow. I mean, that's amazing." His erection throbbed.

"It's not amazing, it's depressing." She picked up the torn section of her nightdress and held it over her bare breast. "I can't figure out what's wrong with me."

"Absolutely nothing is wrong with you. You're the most beautiful woman I've ever met. You're the sweetest—"

"I don't want to be sweet!" Desperation flashed in her eyes. "I want to be wild."

Rick glanced down to where his fierce arousal jutted beneath his untied pajama string. "I think you're well on your way."

"You're shocked."

"In the best possible way." He lifted a thumb and brushed away the tear that ran down her cheek. It broke his heart to see her so sad. "It's a very erotic revelation."

She blinked, her lashes wet. "It is?"

"Absolutely. It means you've never tasted the most

intense sensations in the whole world, and you're about to experience them for the first time."

Her eyes widened. "I am?"

"Absolutely." He leaned in and pressed his lips to hers. They parted, warm and yielding. His tongue flicked into her mouth and he felt her shiver in response.

Gently, he pushed aside the hand covering her breast and replaced it with his own. Her nipple peaked beneath his palm, and sent a flash of heat straight to his groin.

He stroked her nipple with his thumb as he pulled back from the kiss. Her tears had vanished, leaving her eyes bright and curious.

"That feels good," she whispered. She bit her lip, suddenly shy.

"Excellent." He lowered his mouth to her breast and blew. The nipple tightened in response.

"Ooooh," she murmured, arching her back.

He licked a circle around the areola and drank in her rich, feminine scent as he tasted the honeyed silk of her skin.

She rocked against him when he took her nipple in his mouth and sucked. Then he slid the second strap of her nightgown over her shoulder and placed his palm on her other lush, full breast.

Under his fingers, her heartbeat was rapid with excitement.

The soft fabric of her lace-edged nightgown—appropriately virginal—slid down to her waist and he kissed her belly.

His own arousal was excruciating. Everything down there was so sensitive the mere touch of Alicia's manicured hand could send him to another dimension. He really shouldn't be so turned on by her innocence, but something about it was insanely hot.

Gently, he pushed her back against the pillows where she'd so recently tossed and turned in anguish. Her smooth hair splayed on the pillow like a halo. A smile flickered across her full lips as her eyes closed.

She obviously felt safe with him.

Little did she know he was not Rick Jones, the man she trusted with her virtue.

Guilt snaked through him and knotted up with the lust that had overtaken every synapse. He certainly couldn't tell her *now,* while they were locked in a sensual embrace.

Her first.

He slid one hand under her sensational backside and lifted her hips enough to pull her nightgown to her thighs and down over her shapely legs.

"Are you cold?" he whispered.

"Not even a little," she said through a smile. Her thick lashes flickered open and she reached up her arms. "Come here."

He hesitated. While not exactly romantic, a condom was still a necessity. "I'm aching to, but first I have to get something. Don't move a single muscle. Do you promise me you won't?"

"I promise." A slight frown played over her smooth brow.

Rick climbed off the bed and sped to the bathroom and back in record-breaking time. He was half-afraid Alicia would come to her senses and refasten the lock on her chastity belt.

Relief washed over him when he saw her still lying

there, a goddess glazed with moonlight, staring up at him with hungry eyes.

He rolled the condom over his hard length and climbed on to the bed next to her. His hand played over the curve of her hip and her soft belly. She bucked as he slid a finger between her legs and touched the sensitive flesh there. Already hot and slick, she was aroused and ready.

He suppressed a moan of anticipation. He couldn't wait to be inside all that lush heat and enjoy the deep closeness with Alicia.

It's her first time, take it slow.

He drew in a breath and kissed her belly as her fingers ruffled his hair. Her skin quivered as he moved his fingers over her aroused and swollen flesh. Carefully, he parted her legs and lowered his mouth, greedy for the taste of her.

He groaned at the feel of her moist warmth against his mouth. He ran his tongue over her soft folds and she shuddered in response. "Oh, my," she moaned.

A grin crossed his lips as he repeated the gesture. It had been many years since he'd first discovered the unique and tantalizing joys of sex for the first time, but it was a wicked thrill reexperiencing them through Alicia.

Her hips writhed, and she pressed herself against his mouth, begging for more. He licked and sucked until he felt her throb, hot and willing.

Layering kisses over her belly and breasts, he rose over her. He feathered a single, soft kiss on her cheek. "Are you ready?"

She nodded, eyes shut tight as a lascivious smile played over her sensual mouth.

Careful and slow, he guided himself inside. A

breathy groan escaped his mouth when he sank into the hot, tight sweetness of her.

Alicia let out a tiny cry and his eyes flicked open, but instead of pain, her expression spoke of sweet relief.

"I'm free." A broad smile lit her beautiful face.

"And this is just the beginning."

He buried his face in her neck as her hips rose to meet him, drawing him deeper. He built a rhythm and Alicia rode it with him, rising and falling, her breath coming faster and her sweet sighs building to urgent moans.

Celibate for so long, her body was rigged with explosive desire and ready to blow.

And right now, so was his.

Not yet, he pleaded with himself. He couldn't remember feeling such intense and urgent arousal. *It's her first time, make it last.*

Alicia pressed hurried kisses over his face and shoulders, nipping and licking. Her hands pressed his hips to hers, deepening the connection until he could hardly stand it.

Her moans now ended in fevered shrieks, each driving him closer and closer to the brink of insanity.

Suddenly, her fingernails dug into his back. "Ohhh…. Ohhh…."

She shuddered hard as the first waves of her orgasm hit her. The fierce contractions of her untried muscles gripped him and he climaxed with her, riding the waves until they both washed up, sweaty and breathless, on the rumpled shores of her bed.

Eventually, he managed to crack his eyes open. Alicia lay sprawled against the fluffy pillows, hair damp with perspiration.

Her skin glowed golden in the half-light and her chest rose and fell in unsteady gasps.

"Goodness," she breathed.

"I'm not sure goodness has anything to do with it." He winked. "But it's kind of fun, don't you think?"

Alicia let out a laugh that filled the air like sweet music. "Yes!" she shouted. "It's magnificent. Is it true? Am I really no longer a virgin?" Her eyes, wide with humor and excitement, glowed in the darkness.

"You are officially deflowered."

"Thank goodness!"

Justin laughed. "Some women treat their virginity like a prize."

"And I used to be one of them—more fool me." Her pretty white teeth shone in her smile. "Seriously, I'm happy for women who want to have sex for the first time with their husbands, and I'm sure that works great if you marry at…oh, eighteen, but waiting until you're twenty-six? I wouldn't wish that on anyone."

She blew out a hearty sigh. "Did you know that in the Middle Ages they thought prolonged virginity could turn a woman's skin green?"

"Sounds like the ploy of some young swain to get the key to his love's chastity belt."

Her bright gaze filled his heart with joy. "Sex is healthy and normal, not some weird sinful activity that should only be done in the dark while you hold your nose."

"I couldn't agree more." He kissed her soft cheek.

"All those years I was told to keep my legs crossed, *or else*. I didn't know any better."

"Isn't that the whole point of convent school?"

She giggled. "Pretty much, yes. Though it's also a good place to learn how to smoke and drink so that no one smells it on your breath."

"You smoked?"

"No, of course not. I'm the original Goody Two-shoes, remember?"

He cocked his head, then gave her nipple a swift suck. It formed a hard peak. "I'm not so sure."

"Oh, you have no idea what a relief it is to get that millstone off my neck. I feel like a regular person now. I can walk down the street without wondering whether people somehow *know* I'm different."

"I hate to break it to you, but you're definitely not a regular person." He pressed a kiss to her lips. "For one thing, you're dangerously beautiful, so most men are probably afraid to come near you. It takes an especially arrogant one like me to get up the nerve."

She laughed, her full breasts bumping against his chest in a way that made him hard all over again.

"For another, you're brainy as well as beautiful, which is doubly intimidating." He narrowed his eyes. "Except to a genius like myself."

"So modest."

He grinned. "You're anything but ordinary and a run-of-the-mill guy would never cut it for you."

She released a soft, sweet sigh. "Lucky thing I met you, then."

Alicia's radiant, dark eyes shimmered with joy. He'd put that joy there, and it gave him almost as much of a thrill as having sex with her.

There was something truly special about Alicia. She

took pride and pleasure in everything she did, with the result that being around her made a man want to be a better person.

He certainly wanted to be a better person.

Better than a guy who'd give a woman a fake name.

Justin blew out a breath. He *really* wished he'd had a chance to tell her before they'd had sex.

What kind of a cad took the virginity of a woman who had no idea who he truly was?

And she had no clue he was good friends with her brother's longtime rivals. That alone was cause for a big blowup.

He shoved a hand through his hair. He hadn't planned it this way at all.

"Kiss me." Alicia's sweet command blew his labored thoughts from his brain.

He kissed her, enjoying the softness of her mouth and the caress of her hands on his back.

He'd never met a situation he couldn't charm his way out of eventually. He'd figure out the perfect moment to tell her, and everything would be fine.

She'd probably find it funny.

Wouldn't she?

Four

Alicia had trouble opening her eyes. This room was much brighter than her bedroom at home.

It must have been a dream.

A glance to the side confirmed that she lay alone in bed.

But why did her body feel so…strange? Her limbs were heavy, and her breasts seemed more tender than usual. Her lips tingled and so did her…

Goodness. Alicia clutched the covers around her.

Maybe it wasn't a dream.

She turned to look at the pillow beside her in the king-size bed.

The fluffy goose down wrapped in snow-white Egyptian cotton bore the unmistakable indent of a head.

Had she really slept with Rick?

She remembered a dream about being an eighty-year-old virgin.

But she also remembered a second dream.

A glorious dream where Rick kissed her and licked her, his hands roaming over her body until he entered her and drove her to heights of wild pleasure.

Sense memory throbbed in the muscles deep inside her.

Alicia drew in a deep breath as a secret smile spread across her mouth. *It was real*.

But where was Rick?

She pulled on a flowered silk robe and checked her hair in the mirror. Wild, in a sensual kind of way. She fluffed it with her fingers, then opened the door into the hallway.

Bright morning sunlight filled the space. Then she saw the note on her door.

Morning, beautiful, I've gone to a meeting. I'll be back by eleven so don't go anywhere, please—Rick.

His underlined *please* made her laugh. He really wanted her.

If memory served her correctly, he'd enjoyed last night every bit as much as she had. She could almost hear his urgent moans and feel his hot breath on her ear.

A shiver of longing rippled through her and she prayed eleven o'clock wasn't too far away. A peek at the clock in her room answered her prayer. Thank goodness it was Saturday, otherwise she'd have slept through half a morning's work.

Her cell phone rang on the dresser in the bedroom and she hurried to answer it. Her heart pounded and she hoped it was Rick.

"Halloooooo," Maria said.

Could she really give her friend the scoop she'd be sure to insist on?

"Hi, Maria, how are you?"

"Very formal, hmm. Does this mean you were up late last night reading theological philosophy with Mr. Rick Jones?"

Alicia cleared her throat. "Something like that." She was glad Maria couldn't see her guilty smile.

"So, did you guys figure out how many angels can fit on the head of a pin? I've been struggling with that one for years."

Alicia laughed. She could totally picture Maria's raised brow. "We figured about forty, as long as their wings were folded."

Maria tut-tutted. "Come on now, Alicia. Stop playing with me. Did you, or didn't you?"

Alicia hesitated, glanced over her shoulder, then whispered, "We did."

"I knew it!" Maria's joyous whoop almost deafened her. "Well, this calls for a celebration. Want to meet me at T.J.'s for lunch?"

"Actually, Rick's just gone to a meeting and he'll be back by eleven."

"And let me guess. You'd rather have lunch with some new hunk than with your oldest and dearest friend?"

"Well…"

"You'd better! You know I'd ditch you in a second for the right guy."

They both laughed. It was so true.

"Now that we've established that I have no principles, you'd better tell me all the details so I don't rat you out to Alex."

"Alex! Oh, my gosh, I totally forgot about him. He's all alone at the ranch." Guilt pricked her like a needle.

"All alone? You've got at least ten different employees living there."

"You know what I mean. Who'll make him breakfast?"

"He's a big boy. I'm sure he can pour himself a bowl of Wheaties."

"What if the arsonist came back? I've got to call him."

"Not until you tell me more about last night."

"Maria! I'll tell you all about it another time. And believe me, I really appreciate you covering for me, otherwise nothing would have happened at all."

"Okay, okay, but one thing before you cut me off." Maria had stopped teasing and her voice was filled with concern. "I know I joke around a lot, but this Rick Jones better treat my very best friend like a princess or he's going to have me to answer to. Did he make it wonderful for you?"

Alicia nodded, then realized her friend couldn't see. "Oh, Maria, it was more than wonderful. He was so gentle, so tender. It was…beautiful."

"Phew." Maria laughed. "Well, then enjoy your day with him and wish him all the best from me. And give me a call if you want to come up for air."

Alicia shut off her phone and caught sight of her face in the bamboo-framed mirror on the dressing table. Her goofy grin almost made her laugh.

Then she remembered Alex, and her grin vanished.

She punched in his number and waited while the phone rang, cold anxiety trickling through her.

"Hey, 'Manita. How's Maria?"

Alicia gulped. "She's great. How are things at the ranch?" Her voice sounded nervous and false. She hoped he wouldn't press for details about Mária. She didn't want this lie to get any more elaborate.

"No more trouble. The vet's been out to check the animals and the insurance guy was here. The police have interviewed all the workers, but I don't think they have any leads yet."

"I'm coming home, then."

Even as she said it, her entire body screamed *no*. She wanted to stay here, with Rick.

"No way. You stay with Maria. We still have no idea who's behind this, so there's no way to predict what they'll do next. I've got enough problems already. I don't want to have to worry about my baby sister being in danger."

Alicia's relief mingled with stone-cold guilt. "Are you sure you're okay? Did you eat breakfast?"

"I'm not an invalid."

"Did you eat breakfast?"

"I wasn't hungry."

"Alejandro Montoya, you'd better go make yourself something—"

"Stop fussing. Maybe it's better I learn to do things for myself, otherwise how will I manage when you leave to get married?"

His teasing tone told her he was joking. He probably didn't think she'd ever leave to get married. And until this morning, she'd worried the same thing.

But now everything was different.

She fingered her blue topaz necklace and let her smile return. "All right, don't eat anything, then. See if I care."

Her reflection in the mirror revealed red lips and flushed cheeks. Her eyes were glassy and her hair—

well, her hair needed work. "I'll call you later and you can reach me on my cell if you need me."

She hung up the phone. How shocked Alex would be if he knew what she'd been up to last night. If he knew that—right now—she was waiting for her new boyfriend to return.

Her lover.

Finally.

Justin marched up the walkway into the Texas Cattleman's Club. Things were getting too complicated for his taste and he intended to do a little untangling. At least as much as he could without making Alicia run for cover.

"Good afternoon, Mr. Dupree." The doorman nodded to him. "Mr. Brody's waiting for you in the library."

"Justin!" Mitch rose from a leather club chair near the carved-stone fireplace as Justin entered, his dark eyes shining with amusement. "You've been hard to find lately."

"Busy. We're in the midst of a deal. I'm wearing a suit right now because I just signed a contract. Saturday morning, can you believe it? But the guy's heading back to Athens this afternoon."

His tall friend narrowed his eyes. "That's not the only thing keeping you tied up. I saw how well you hit it off with Alicia Montoya."

Justin just smiled.

"Did you dig up any dirt on her brother?" Mitch asked.

Guilt trickled through Justin as he eased himself into

a chair. He wished he'd never volunteered to get information about Alex from Alicia.

Both Mitch and his brother, Lance, suspected Alex of the sabotage at Brody Oil and Gas, but because of the longtime enmity between Lance and Alex, there was no way they could approach him without things quickly escalating to a confrontation. It happened every time Lance and Alex got near each other.

"Pretty suspicious that a fire broke out on the Montoya place, don't you think?" Mitch asked.

"They don't know who's behind the fire at El Diablo. The police are looking into it but there are no suspects yet, from what I hear."

"Do you think it's possible that Alex set the fire to divert suspicion from himself about the fire at our refinery?"

"Why would he destroy his own property?"

"For the insurance money." Mitch took a sip of whiskey. "That old barn was begging to be burned down. He probably had it insured for twice its value."

"Alicia said it was a historic building. One of the oldest in Somerset."

"Maybe they wanted to clear the way for a state-of-the-art setup. Alex has some of the finest breeding cattle in the entire state of Texas these days. He always was a competitive son of a bitch." Mitch signaled to the bartender to bring a drink for Justin.

"I don't think he's behind it."

Mitch looked at Justin closely. "Who else could it be?"

Justin leaned back in his chair. "It's got me stumped. But I'm starting to think that the fires are somehow tied into the missing funds Darius discovered. Have you finished the unofficial audit yet?"

"Not yet," said Mitch, "but I'm close."

"Look, Mitch, from what Alicia's told me, the refinery fire doesn't sound like something Alex would do. He's a legitimate businessman."

"One of his best buddies is Paul Rodriquez. Don't try to tell me 'El Gato' is legit."

"No, El Gato has 'drug cartel' written all over him, but he and Alex Montoya aren't business partners. They're old friends or something. Alex has an import-export business, and from the sounds of it, he's making money at the ranch, too, with those big-ticket bulls he's breeding."

A wry smile lifted one side of Mitch's mouth. "Are you falling for Alicia Montoya?"

Justin took a gulp of whiskey. "I'm telling you what I've learned. The Montoyas seem like decent and up-standing people. I think we've all been too hasty in our judgment of Alex."

Mitch took a swig from his own glass. "He slammed the brakes on redeveloping downtown and ruined Kevin's deal. One of the councillors told me he was so persuasive that he almost single-handedly talked the city council into rezoning the area for historic develop-ment. I can't figure out if he actually wants to redevelop it himself, or if he just couldn't stand to see someone else make a buck doing it."

"Alicia's heavily involved in the preservation of the downtown area. She says it's one of the few authentic and picturesque main streets in the state. She's working on a committee to turn it into a tourist attraction."

"*Downtown* Somerset as a tourist attraction? I

suspect you're thinking with a part of your body other than your brain."

"Why not? If you look past the cheesy signage and faded paint, there are some beautiful buildings there. I think she's absolutely right to want to preserve Somerset's history. We already have enough strip malls in the Houston suburbs."

"It's hard to argue with that." Mitch peered into his glass. "As I get older, I'm starting to take a more serious interest in the future and what will be here when my own children grow up."

Justin's eyes widened. "Are you and Lexi already talking about children?"

Mitch smiled slyly. "We've done more than talk about it. We're expecting."

Justin almost choked on his drink. He'd been shocked to his boot heels when Mitch said he was getting married. Mitch was always the last man standing at the bar and the first to run from any sign of a woman wanting commitment.

Apparently Alexis Cavanaugh—now Alexis Brody—had worked some kind of magic spell on him.

"That's great. Congratulations."

"You're pole-axed." Mitch's smile broadened into a grin.

"Totally."

"I don't blame you. I used to laugh at the whole idea of love and marriage, let alone family. But let me tell you, when you meet the right woman, your whole world changes."

Justin blinked. He'd certainly been looking at things differently since he met Alicia. Lying about his name, for example. He wasn't going to do that again—ever.

"With Lexi, did you just…know?"

Mitch blew out a sigh. "It was a bit more complicated than that. You know the story. It started out as a business arrangement with Senator Cavanaugh. She was supposed to marry Lance. When Lance ruined that plan by marrying Kate, I figured I'd marry Lexi myself. Then I fell madly in love with her."

"Sounds like a real fairy tale—Texas style." Justin raised his glass and laughed.

"I'll drink to that. You're next, bro. I have a feeling." Mitch's dark eyes narrowed. "And from the way you're defending the Montoya family, I'm beginning to wonder if you've already met your lady. I bet Alex wouldn't mind his sister marrying into the illustrious Dupree clan."

"Yeah, except for the fact that the Brodys are my best friends. He doesn't know I'm seeing her."

"She's keeping you as her dirty little secret?"

"Something like that."

"Well, watch your back. There are strange things going on all around us."

"Too true. If the Brody brothers can settle down and get married, almost anything can happen."

"Fires are burning, bro. Fires are burning. Sometimes they start right here." Mitch tapped his chest with a knuckle. "When that happens, there's no way to put 'em out."

The click of the lock made Alicia jump to her feet. She'd had plenty of time to shower and style her hair and put on one of her favorite dresses—which just happened to match the necklace Rick gave her.

And if he were to look underneath her dress—an event she fervently hoped for—he'd find a pretty lace bra and panties in a contrasting shade of pale blue.

"Alicia." Rick's warm, masculine voice sent a shiver of awareness through her.

"I'm here." She hurried out into the hallway, heart pounding.

Rick stopped, as if struck motionless by the sight of her. He looked devastatingly handsome in a stylish, dark gray suit. His hair was tousled and his blue eyes sparkled with fascination.

He held out a bouquet of fat pink roses. "I bought these for you." He frowned. "But I want you holding me, not a bunch of roses." He glanced around for a surface to put them down on, then set them gently on a hall table. "Much better. Now my hands are free."

Alicia's body shimmered with anticipation as Rick took a bold step toward her. Her eyes closed as he wrapped his strong arms around her and gave her a tender kiss on the lips.

Pleasure crept over her like the sun's heat. Her nipples thickened against the stiff fabric of his suit. And hidden, secret parts of her—parts she'd never been fully aware of—now throbbed with desire.

He grew hard against her, and she instinctively pressed her hips against his erection, delighting in the arousal that flared between them.

"Damn, I missed you so much." His voice was rough.

"You were only gone for a couple of hours."

"Way too long. Let's not do that again anytime soon." He pulled off his slim dark tie with two fingers and unbuttoned the collar of his white shirt to reveal his bronzed neck.

On impulse, Alicia slipped her fingers into the collar of his shirt, against his hot skin.

Rick kissed her nose, which made her smile. Her fingers—without checking back to her brain—unbuttoned the next button on his shirt, and the next, while her other hand slid over the rippling muscle of his pecs.

The scent of him drove her half-crazy. The fine wool of his expensive suit mingled with the musky aroma of sexually aroused male—an inviting combination of civilized and primitive.

She raked her nails over the front of his crisp shirt, down past his sleek, leather belt, to the thick bulge beneath it.

Rick groaned as she wrapped her hand around his rigid length through his pants. She held him, tight, while she let her other hand rest on the firm curve of his athletic backside.

He grew harder still when she freed her hands to pluck at his belt buckle.

Her breath came in unsteady gasps as desire pounded inside her like a drum, heightened by Rick's obvious excitement.

His hands roamed over her silky dress, strumming her nipples and exploring the curve of her waist.

At last, she freed the leather from the buckle and tugged down the zipper. His erection throbbed against her hand and made her shiver.

Without ceremony, she shoved down his pants and

pressed herself against his thick arousal. She couldn't wait to feel him inside her.

Rick lifted the skirt of her dress and slid a bold hand inside her panties. Hot and slick, she writhed against him.

"Take me now. Right here," she breathed, hardly aware of her own words.

Rick's erection throbbed again. He pulled a condom from his jacket pocket, ripped it open with his teeth and rolled it on. Then he tugged her panties to one side and entered her.

Alicia cried out at the intense sensation, then gripped Rick so her scream wouldn't make him back away.

Rick cupped her buttocks and lifted her up to him until her back arched and she took him as deep as she could.

"Oh, yes, just like that. It feels so good," she murmured, rocking against him.

Sensation swirled through her, and colors flashed behind her eyelids. She clung to Rick, her fingers clutching his rapidly dampening shirt.

She hadn't even given him time to remove his jacket. A burst of laughter accompanied the thought.

"What's so funny?"

"Me," she said on a groan as she writhed against him. "I couldn't wait for us to get undressed. I wore pretty underwear and you didn't even get to see it."

Her breasts felt swollen and deliciously sensitive against their lacy prison.

"Let me have a look," rasped Rick.

Keeping the steady rhythm, he raised a hand and tugged down the front of her dress.

"Nice." He flashed a dazzling blue gaze that made her heart leap. "Sometimes it's more fun to do things out of order."

She gasped as he lifted her feet off the floor and strode for the living room, still hard inside her.

Without missing a beat, he eased them both down onto a green silk chaise lounge.

Alicia's eyes squeezed shut as he thrust into her, but not before she had time to take in the restrained elegance of the setting: expensive antiques, fine china and crystal, delicate watercolor paintings.

What they were doing here seemed so *wrong*.

In the best possible way.

She wriggled under him, enjoying the sound of her own pleasured moans. "Oh, yes, Rick, again. Do it again." She clutched him to her as he rode her until every nerve and muscle of her body hummed with sheer bliss.

Just when she was about to lose all control—

He stopped.

Completely stopped. No movement at all, except their chests rising and falling against each other as their breath came in ragged gulps.

She tried to lift her hips but the sheer weight of his muscled body made it impossible.

Almost growling with frustrated desire, she opened her eyes, and saw his dangerous baby blues staring at her. A wicked smile slid across his mouth.

"What?" she gasped, her body sprung like a catapult and desperate for release.

"Good things come to those who wait," he whispered.

Alicia wiggled, which had no result but to make her

more agonizingly aroused. When she was about to scream, he started to move again.

Oh. So. Slowly.

Only the tiniest movements at first. Incremental. Just enough to drive her that little bit closer to the brink of insanity.

He slid—very gently—in and out, the stroking motion creating an extraordinary sensation.

Then he picked up speed.

Alicia moaned and cried out with relief as she built toward her climax. The pressure intensified, growing and gathering inside her like a huge storm cloud ready to explode and drench the whole state.

Her orgasm crashed over her like a clap of thunder, sucking the breath from her lungs and throwing her back against the chaise lounge with a howl of exuberant release.

Rick's own climax shook him like a jackhammer and he cried out as he collapsed on top of her.

It was some moments before she managed to draw enough breath to speak. "What was that? What were you doing?"

"Have you ever heard of the G-spot?"

"I think I read about it in *Cosmo* once."

"Well—" a naughty grin lifted one side of his mouth "—now you know what it does."

She lay splayed over the chaise, her head hanging slightly off one end so her hair brushed the floor. Rick held her on to the silk surface with a firm arm, or she might have fallen limply to the carpet.

Alicia blinked. "G-spot, huh?" Her muscles still throbbed with stray contractions. "I wonder what evolutionary purpose that serves."

Rick chuckled. "The natural historian at work. Isn't pleasure reason enough for it to exist?"

"I suppose." She pressed a thoughtful finger to her lips. "I could see how once you've experienced that, you'd keep coming back for more, which would likely ensure the survival of your genes in the next generation."

"Unless you're using a condom." Rick traced a line on her belly with his finger. Her muscles shivered in response.

"So true. In that case, you have to admit you're doing it just for fun."

They both chuckled. Then Alicia's stomach grumbled.

"Hey, did you have breakfast?"

"No. I confess. I was distracted by my other appetites." With some effort, she lifted her head up onto the chaise. "And I even berated Alex for not eating properly this morning. I'm such a hypocrite."

Rick's playful expression faded. "You spoke to Alex?"

"Yes. I wanted to make sure everything was okay at the ranch."

"Did you tell him you're here?"

"No." She shifted onto her elbow. "It's better he doesn't know, especially with so much going on. He'll just worry, then overreact."

"And I'll be challenged to pistols at dawn for assailing your virtue."

"Exactly." Alicia sighed. "Why go looking for drama? Let's at least wait until they find out who set the fire. Then he'll have some other man to direct his hostile energies toward."

Five

"Where are we going?" Alicia asked as Justin pulled onto the freeway. They'd changed their clothing after the impromptu tryst, then headed right out in search of lunch.

"Downtown Somerset."

He could feel her curious gaze on him. "Why?"

"Because I want to see it through your eyes." Since he was now striding around town defending her plan to preserve the old buildings, he wanted to know more about what he was trying to save.

And more about the lovely Alicia.

Her gaze darkened. "What if Alex sees us?"

He managed not to laugh. "Is he likely to be hanging around downtown Somerset on a Saturday afternoon?" For someone so smart, she was more than a little paranoid.

"Well, no, but…"

"So stop worrying. If we run into him you can say I'm a visiting professor of natural history," he said, knowing full well that if they did run into Alex, she wouldn't be the only one who had some explaining to do.

She chuckled. "There is no such thing. Besides, you don't look like a professor." She eyed the pale blue shirt he'd changed into. "They don't usually wear Prada."

"Me, either. It was a gift from one of my aunts."

"She has good taste. I like the color."

He smiled. "I know. That's why I wore it. See? I'm getting to know you, bit by bit. And so far, I haven't found a bit I don't like."

"All this talk about biting is making me squirm." She wriggled in her seat, inadvertently pulling her simple white dress tight across her full chest.

Justin suppressed a groan of arousal. "Please, don't talk about biting and squirming while I'm driving. It could be dangerous."

Alicia let out a little growl. The lascivious gesture sent a ripple of lust straight up his spine. He couldn't wait to see more of her wild side.

Alicia crossed her sleek, tanned legs, giving him a flash of inner thigh.

The sensation in his crotch was getting to be pretty unbearable. "Tell me where to park," he said as he pulled off at the exit. The hum and buzz of Houston subsided as they entered the peaceful, tree-lined streets of historic Somerset.

Victorian houses sat gracefully amidst large lawns and mature trees. A kid rode by on a bike, like something out of the 1950s.

"That house is a Stanford White." She pointed to a stunning Beaux Arts "cottage" he'd never noticed before. "He was a famous nineteenth-century architect who—"

"Was murdered by the husband of a woman he had a scandalous affair with."

"You've heard of him," she said with surprise and delight in her eyes.

"I had one of the most expensive educations money can buy. Despite that, I managed to pick up a few facts along the way. It's a beautiful house."

He'd stopped the car and they sat with the engine humming. "The detail is incredible. You'd never see that kind of elaborate molding on a house today."

"And just two years ago it was condemned. The roof was damaged during a storm and the city wanted to tear it down. That's when I joined the Somerset Historical Society and we raised money to have it restored."

Pride showed on her beautiful face. "It sold for two million when it was finished, and the owner loves it so much, she lets us give tours as a fundraiser."

Justin was intrigued. "How did you get interested in architectural history?"

"I always loved to look at beautiful houses." She glanced up at the steep eaves and shimmering multi-paned windows. "When I was a little girl we lived in a tiny house in the barrio. The roof leaked and the foundation was half-rotted, but my parents didn't dare ask the landlord to fix anything in case he tried to raise the rent. My parents saved every penny they had because they couldn't wait to move out of there and buy their own home. The American dream, you know?"

She laughed, but her laughter was tinged with sorrow. "They used to talk so much about that house they dreamed of—the sunny windows it would have with views of a grassy backyard, a big kitchen with rows of shining copper pots. Alex wanted his own bedroom so he could put up shelves for his collection of model airplanes."

For a second, her eyes filled with tears. "I don't suppose they ever came close to having enough money for a down payment. My dad was killed in an accident where he worked and after that my mom just struggled to make ends meet. No one talked much about buying a house again. Except Alex." She smiled. "He always said you have to dream big, no matter what. Even after our mother died, he kept saying that."

"He's right." Emotion rose in Justin's chest.

How he wished he could turn back time and give Alicia's family the house of their dreams. The most pressing financial problem his parents ever faced was finding new tax loopholes to exploit.

He slid his arm around her shoulder. "Your parents would be so happy to see you and Alex at El Diablo."

"Oh, I know." Her eyes brightened. "My mom used to clean houses all over Somerset and El Diablo was one of them. She took such pleasure in polishing all the lovely quarter-sawn oak trim and buffing the brass doorknobs." She stared out the window, as if lost in the past. "I know this sounds silly, but when we were there—she used to take me along when school was out because she couldn't afford a sitter—we'd pretend it was all ours. I used to dance down those corridors and pretend one of those pretty bedrooms with the chintz curtains was mine, and that I had a closet filled with fine clothes."

"And now you do."

"Yeah." A broad grin settled across her face as she turned to him. "Funny, isn't it?"

"It's totally awesome," he said, meaning every word of it. "I guess the American dream is alive and well in Somerset." He squeezed Alicia and she nuzzled against him.

Something kicked inside his heart. A fierce longing to give Alicia the world—or at least the most beautiful house in it.

Where did that come from?

"So, there are more of these old gems in Somerset?"

"Oh, yes. It developed as a suburb for wealthy Houstonians, so nearly all of the buildings are special in some way. Look at this one."

She pointed to a quasi-gothic stone structure across the street. "The owner fell in love with a medieval abbey in Somerset, England, and had it brought here brick by brick and rebuilt as his home. It even has some of the original stained glass inside. I gave a tour of it last year through the museum."

"You're a busy woman."

"Keeps me out of trouble." She flashed him a grin.

"Until now." He grazed her neck with his teeth. Desire flashed through him, and he realized they were still idling on a busy street. "But let's save that energy for later."

"Sounds like a plan. Can we stop by Julie's Gems so I can rave over her work on the necklace you gave me?"

"Sure thing." He couldn't hide a pleased grin as he pulled back on to the road, heading for Main Street, the focus of Alicia's preservation efforts.

He hoped they wouldn't run into anyone who'd greet him as Justin. On the other hand, if they did, maybe it would be the hand of fate at work.

Alicia showed him a hidden alleyway behind Julie's Gems where his car barely fit into the single parking space. "You need more parking around here," he muttered with a raised brow.

Alicia shrugged. "Or more people need to start using public transportation." She winked. "It's better for the earth."

"This is Texas, sweetheart."

"So? Miracles can happen." She smiled sweetly and marched ahead of him up the neat alley. Her heels clicked authoritatively over the cobblestones. The way her backside jiggled slightly inside her flimsy white dress almost deprived him of his senses.

Miracles can happen.

With Alicia around, he had a feeling almost anything could happen.

"I can't wait to thank Julie for the work she did on this topaz." She opened the door. "I think it's the loveliest gift I've ever had."

Justin followed her into the store and greeted Julie. "It was a hit."

"I knew it would be." The bubbly jeweler hurried from behind the counter and gave Alicia a hug. "But you didn't tell me it was for one of my favorite people."

Justin shrugged. "I didn't know you two knew each other."

"Alicia knows everyone in Somerset," said Julie, tossing her red curls. "And we all adore her."

Alicia flushed sweetly.

Julie stared at the topaz glittering on the delicate chain around her lovely neck. "And that is some very fine craftsmanship, if I do say so myself. Though I do have to give some credit to Rick for bringing me such a perfect stone. I don't believe for a minute that he dug it up himself." She shot him a wry glance. "But he certainly has an eye for a fine gem."

Justin chuckled. "I was with an experienced rock hound. Otherwise I probably would have tossed it back into the soil."

Julie narrowed her eyes at Alicia. "Do you believe a word of this?"

"I do." Alicia's sweet smile and words of affirmation filled Justin's chest with warmth.

Until he remembered that she had every reason to be wary of him.

Would she believe his story about the stone if she knew he wasn't Rick Jones? He'd used the fake name here, too, as he often did when he didn't want the media sniffing after him.

He'd gotten so tired of stories and innuendo— *Shipping Heir Commissions Jewels for Mystery Sweetheart*—that subterfuge was second nature to him now.

Would Alicia have treated him differently if he'd introduced himself as Justin Dupree?

For all he knew, Alicia had never heard of the Duprees.

She'd figured out by now that he was well-off—a four-bedroom penthouse hotel suite let that cat out of the bag—but she hadn't asked where the money came from.

She seemed to genuinely enjoy his company and showed no interest in plumbing the depth of his pockets.

Most girls would be fingering the sparkling bracelets—or rings—by now, in the hope that he'd offer to buy her another, but Alicia was far from the velvet-lined cases, chatting enthusiastically with Julie about her plans to restore the downtown area.

"Julie did a lot of the restoration on this storefront herself."

"I live in the apartment above it, too," Julie said, gesturing to the patterned tin ceiling. "I love everything about this area. I'm so glad it's not going to be bulldozed and turned into a parking lot."

"At least not if Alex and I can keep stalling the developers." Alicia sighed. "Some people don't think about anything but money."

"I wish there were more people like you and your brother, who don't mind standing up to the powers that be."

Alicia chuckled. "We've been doing it our whole lives, so we're not going to stop now. And once people start to see what downtown Somerset can be, they'll all jump on the bandwagon and congratulate themselves for coming up with the idea."

Julie laughed. "She's the eternal optimist."

"Yet another reason why she deserves only the best. And she also needs some lunch, rather urgently. Julie, would you care to join us?"

"Heck no." Julie crossed her arms. "You two need to be alone. And you need to get out of here before all the chemistry in the air starts turning my gems pink."

Alicia giggled, which made her full breasts bounce

against the white fabric of her dress. Justin tried to ignore the heat rising in his groin.

He shot Julie a grin. "Thanks again, Julie. You're a gem."

"Yeah. I hear that all the time." She crossed her arms over her chest and shot him a knowing smile. "If you dig up any more AAA quality rocks, you know who to call."

Her wink told him she still didn't believe his story—which was in fact the gospel truth. As usual, he didn't care in the least whether she believed him or not. He'd never been one to sweat other people's opinions—until he met Alicia.

"I thought we'd go to Tea and Sympathy for some lunch," he said in her ear as they left the shop. The honey scent of her skin made him want to bury his face in her neck, but he managed to restrain himself.

"Perfect." She flashed a pearly grin. "They make smoked salmon and cucumber sandwiches to die for."

"I hope no one will have to die." He couldn't resist grazing his hand down her waist and over the lush curve of her backside as he ushered her under the striped awning over the tea shop.

"Outside or inside?" He nodded at the wrought-iron tables and chairs that lined the slate sidewalk.

"Definitely inside." She glanced up and down the street like a fugitive. "I know it's very unlikely Alex is anywhere near here, but…" She shrugged. "Humor me, please?"

"I'd do anything for you."

The words rattled around his brain as he followed her into the darkest corner of the café and pulled out her chair.

He couldn't remember having feelings like this for

a woman—ever. Usually all his devotion went into the family business, and his free time was spent blowing off steam.

Right now, steam thickened in the air between him and Alicia. It hovered over the white, cotton tablecloth and wound around the wooden chairs. Wisps licked around their fingers as they both reached for the crystal pitcher of water in the center of the table, and their fingers—almost—touched.

His palms prickled with the urge to run over the silky curves of her body. To strip off her soft white dress and watch her skin bead with perspiration as he drove her to new heights of bliss.

This steam was a delicious torment, and he had no desire to blow it off at all.

"Can you believe this storefront was originally built as a tea shop?"

"I can. Our ancestors were mad about tea. I hear they started a war over it once."

Alicia smiled. "The Boston Tea Party happened at least a hundred years before this area was developed. Still, it's reassuring to think that some things have stayed the same. We think we're so advanced with our laptops and cell phones, but deep down, we enjoy the same things our ancestors did."

He'd finished pouring water for both of them and she picked up her glass and took a sip. "Has your family always lived in the Houston area?"

An edge to her voice told him she was becoming increasingly curious about him. As well she might.

"Actually they're not from the Houston area at all. They settled outside New Orleans at the end of the

Pleistocene Era and they're still there today. Well, my mom is. My dad died three years ago."

"I'm sorry to hear that." Sorrow filled her big brown eyes.

"It was a merciful release. He'd been sick for a long time. That's when I took over running the family business."

"What kind of business is it?" She leaned forward.

"Transportation. Did you see they have crumpets on the menu?"

"Rick! You're so mysterious. I'm beginning to be quite suspicious of you. What type of transportation?"

"Ferrying goods from place to place. Container shipping. Very unglamorous, I'm afraid."

He glanced at the printed menu, hoping she'd drop the subject.

Duprees and shipping went together like tea and crumpets. Yes, she had to find out who he was eventually, but he'd prefer to have it happen someplace private, as he expected her reaction might be…dramatic.

"I think it sounds intriguing. So, you import and export goods from all over the world? That's what Alex does."

"Other people import and export them—people like Alex—and they pay money to bring their goods on our ships. We just get the goods from A to B. We used to run everything out of New Orleans, but back in the fifties we moved most of our operations to Houston, which is why I work here."

He tapped his menu. "Hey, they've got quails' eggs. I haven't eaten those in years. I'm definitely having that. How about you?"

Alicia's eyes narrowed. Apparently, she was hip to

his desire to change the subject. "I'll have the egg salad. They make it English style with a dash of curry powder."

"A flash of heat just where you least expect it."

"Exactly." Her plump lips slid into an enticing smile. "I know I'm feeling flashes of heat in all kinds of places I never expected."

Justin leaned forward. "And we've only begun to explore your erogenous zones."

He'd much rather think about Alicia's erogenous zones than the illustrious Dupree clan.

Her eyes widened and she glanced anxiously around the café.

"Don't worry. No one can hear us." He should know. He was used to keeping his affairs private. He'd learned the hard way.

They gave their orders to the friendly waitress, then Alicia leaned in close. "Is your mother lonely now that she's a widow?" Concern filled her beautiful eyes.

Justin startled at the deeply personal question. "Oh, no. She's not the lonely type. Always busy with charitable activities, friends, that kind of thing."

"I'm glad to hear that. I always think it must be so hard to lose your spouse once your children have grown up and left home. Suddenly, you're all on your own."

He stared at Alicia for a moment. His mother probably had never been all on her own in her whole life.

There was a staff of five just inside the house, and at least another ten on the estate. Not to mention that his mother was a blur of motion. When he was little, he used to resent that she never invited him to sit on her lap for a story, the way mothers did in books. She was far too busy for that.

Over time, he got used to it. Maybe that's why he didn't get all misty-eyed over the idea of family life. He'd never really had any. His father was at work all the time, or off participating in manly sporting pursuits.

Quite possibly having affairs as well.

His parents' relationship was anything but romantic. He couldn't imagine how they'd managed to conceive him. Perhaps some aristocratic breeding process involving frozen semen.

"She must wish you lived closer." Alicia tilted her head with sympathy.

"Oh, I'm not so sure. I'd been away at school almost since I'd learned to read. If she was desperate to clutch me to her bosom, she'd have done it a long time ago."

"You didn't grow up at home?"

"Sure, I was there until I turned eight, or so. Then they decided it was time to get serious about my education. I did come home for vacations, though."

"That's horrible! I've never heard of such a thing."

"It's a family tradition. I went to the same school my father attended. The family estate is out in the country so there wasn't really a school for me to go to there."

Not unless he'd attended the local public school— over his mother's dead body. He suppressed a snort. The idea of a Dupree having a normal childhood was quite laughable.

"Would you do that to your child?" Her face was tight with alarm.

"I don't know. I've never thought about it."

"Never? Do you not want children?" She'd pulled

back from the table, almost seeming to put distance between them.

"Sure I do. I think." He frowned. He truly had never thought about it. "I mean, everyone does, sooner or later."

Alicia stared at him like he'd grown alien antennae. "You're thirty years old and you haven't given a moment's thought to starting a family?"

"I'm busy with work." Was that so odd? His crowd didn't talk much about settling down.

Well, not until lately. Suddenly, it was all the rage.

Alicia must think he was some depraved party animal who never looked beyond that evening's festivities. He frowned. "You're right. It is strange. I guess I never met someone who made me think about it."

Until now.

The words hung in the air between them.

"You're used to being alone." She bit her lip. "For all I complain about Alex, I admit I've never really wanted to live alone. I'm used to having my family about me, small as it is."

"I could see how you worried about him being alone even for one day. I think that's sweet."

What would it be like to have someone care that much about you?

He'd been expected to fend for himself from a young age. Part of becoming a man. Or becoming a Dupree. It had never occurred to him before that those two things were different, that you could be a man without being a distant, patrician father who wouldn't kiss his son good-night in case it made him "soft."

"I think there's a lot to be envied and admired about the close relationship between you and Alex. Kind of makes me wish I had a sister I could smother." He shot her a mischievous smile.

"Much as I complain, I know he just does it because he cares. He's a big softy, really, underneath the gruff exterior. I bet you guys will get along great once you get to know each other."

"If you ever allow us to meet, that is," he teased.

The waitress set down their lunch and he watched as Alicia took a bite out of her egg-salad sandwich. She chewed thoughtfully.

"You know what? Maybe it is time for you guys to meet."

Justin froze.

"I mean, we've already been…intimate." Her lovely complexion darkened a shade. "So, he can't exactly forbid me to see you."

"He might just insist we marry before sunset."

Alicia giggled. "You're so right. My honor is at stake." She took a sip of water and flushed even darker. "But don't worry. I don't expect you to marry me just because you've claimed my virtue."

She was embarrassed, but turned on at the same time. Her dark eyes glittered and her lips and cheeks were flushed. Alicia Montoya was apparently much more interested in making wild and passionate love than in securing a big rock for her finger.

There was something very reassuring—and totally hot—about that.

She leaned in. "Come to think of it, I pretty much threw my virtue at you."

"You sure did." His voice was husky, and his pants uncomfortably tight. "Lucky thing I'm a good catch."

"I was so upset when you didn't try anything."

"It practically killed me not to. I had to take a cold shower that night. But after all you'd been through with the fire and the suspicion of arson, I didn't want to take advantage of you." He grinned at her. "I had no idea you were downright desperate to be taken advantage of."

He raised a quail's egg to his mouth and flicked his tongue over it for a second before popping it in.

Alicia's eyes flashed. "I've got a lot of lost time to make up for."

"About ten years, I'd say. We'd better get cracking right after lunch. I'm going to take you to one of my favorite places."

Six

Rick turned the car down a gravel drive and under the scrolled-iron arch leading to the Houston Bay Yacht Club.

Alicia's eyes widened. "I've heard of this club."

She patted her hair. She'd insisted on having the top down so she could enjoy the breeze—now she regretted the rash gesture.

"Whatever you've heard, it's not all that bad."

"Oh, stop it. This is probably the most exclusive yacht club in the world. Don't some of the crowned heads of Europe dock here?"

"Sure. Loads of kings and queens milling about. But we'll do our best to avoid them." He shot her a grin. "I come for the sailing, not the socializing."

"I guess that makes sense if you're in the shipping business."

"A container ship has virtually nothing in common

with a racing yacht, except that they both float on water."

"That's a big thing. I've never been on a boat before."

She wasn't sure if she was excited or terrified at the prospect of floating out on the ocean.

"Really?" Rick turned to her, eyebrows raised.

"I've never been on a cruise, or in a canoe, or even in a rowboat at the park. You probably think that's pretty funny."

Manicured flower beds lined the drive, which ended at a small parking lot hosting an extravagant collection of luxury vehicles.

"I think it's great." Rick's smile broadened as he pulled into a space between an SUV the size of a WWI tank and a vintage Bentley. "Another of life's grandest experiences awaits you."

He jumped out and hurried around to open her door. She couldn't help smiling at the chivalrous gesture. "And I'd be delighted to show you the ropes, literally and figuratively."

"That sounds kinky."

"Good, it was meant to."

He guided her out of the parking lot and up some stone stairs toward an imposing clubhouse. But instead of leading her to the door, he took her elbow and ushered her around the side of the building, through a small garden, and down two more flights of steps to the marina.

Alicia gasped at the sight of all those white boats bobbing like corks in the bright afternoon sun.

"Choppy today," said Rick cheerfully.

Alicia's stomach contracted.

"Always makes it more exciting. Unless I'm trying to clock my best time, then it ticks me off."

"You race?"

"Absolutely." The light glinted off his dark hair as he squinted into the sun. "It's a true rush to race someone else using only the power of the wind to propel you. That's when you learn what you're made of."

Alicia glanced about, suddenly aware of her heeled shoes. "What if I find I'm made of something that melts?"

He slid his arm around her waist and hugged her close. "Don't worry, I'll lick you all up if you melt." His hot whisper made her ear tingle.

"You're so bad!" She tapped his arm, which didn't budge from around her waist.

The sturdy warmth of his muscled embrace buoyed her confidence. "Hey, I always brag about how much I like to try something new. Here I am. Show me the ropes, sailor man."

They walked through the marina, past rows of gleaming yachts and speedboats, ranging in size from the tiniest dingy to luxury cruisers with brass-trimmed decks that looked like you could host a party of a hundred on them.

Rick waved at two tanned preppy types winding a coil of rope on the dock of one of the boats, but he didn't introduce her.

Alicia glanced back at the clubhouse. Sun gleamed on the slate roof and illuminated the stone planters overflowing with yellow flowers. She was curious to see what the place looked like inside.

Maybe Rick just wasn't into the social aspect of

things. Or maybe she wasn't the type of girl he'd show off to his friends.

A chill swept through her. She wasn't some waspy princess with an Ivy League degree and a pedigree dating back to the Mayflower.

Her heels clicked loudly on the decking. Rick marched ahead of her, the muscle of his shoulders flexing under his shirt, past millions of dollars worth of ocean-going hardware.

She couldn't shake a sudden, powerful feeling that she didn't belong here.

"Nearly there. I dock at the end of the marina so I can get in and out without getting stuck behind a bunch of Sunday sailors."

And maybe he wanted to get her on to the yacht and out of the club before anyone could figure out that she wasn't one of them.

Oh, Alicia, you're being silly! Why look for the negative in this beautiful moment?

So what if he wasn't going to marry her and take her home to Mom?

She wasn't here for that. She was here to enjoy a beautiful afternoon with an exciting and thoughtful man, and to have a good time. Not to worry about what was and wasn't going to happen between them in the future.

"There she is." He beamed and pointed at a long, sleek white boat with red sails furled against a tall mast. The letters TITAN III were emblazoned on the side in red.

Alicia looked warily at the shiny white deck. "What happened to Titans one and two?"

"Oh, they're out there in little pieces somewhere.

Luckily, I'm a strong swimmer." A dimple appeared in his cheek as he surveyed her, laughter in his blue eyes.

"You're joking."

"Yes, I'm joking. I sold them when something better came along. I'm fickle like that."

And you'd do well to remember that, young lady, and not get carried away thinking about happily-ever-afters.

Her main goal—humiliating as it was—had been to shed her embarrassing virginity and have a good time doing it. If their relationship continued a bit longer and they had more fun together, so much the better.

Right?

"Ready to board?" He lifted an arm to help her up to the ramp that connected the boat to the dock. "You'll want to take your shoes off when you get on deck. It can be slippery as the boat kicks up some spray once we get going. But don't worry, there's a rope to hang on to."

"Great," managed Alicia, taking tentative steps up the stamped-metal ramp.

She could swim, thanks to lessons under the stern command of Sister Benedict, but she'd never swum anywhere except a chlorinated pool, with no waves or undertow whatsoever.

On the deck, she removed her shoes and handed them to Rick, who stowed them in a cubby.

"Take a seat over there."

Alicia looked. The closest thing to a seat was a slippery-looking ledge. She sat down on the sun-warmed surface while Rick started unwinding rope and unfurling the sails. He tossed her a life jacket and she donned it with some relief.

"I love to come out here," he said cheerfully.

"There's no better way to shake off the petty concerns and stresses of the business world than to set out to sea with wind in your face."

The wind whipped the pale cotton of her dress against her skin, where it clung to her curves. Sunlight glistened off her legs and toasted her bare feet, while the water sparkled all around them.

Beautiful.

Finished with the sail, Rick unwound the rope tying them to the dock and pushed away from the ramp.

Alicia watched, riveted, as he guided the yacht out into the bay using the tiller and movements of the sails, and a lot of taut and tanned muscle. The memory of those strong arms around her made her belly quiver as she saw him work.

He was a very capable man with a surprising array of talents. She couldn't help glowing with pride that of all the women in the world, he'd chosen to spend the afternoon with her.

What did it matter if he didn't want to introduce her to his yacht-club buddies?

They were probably boring anyway.

She turned her face to the sun and let it warm her. She'd been spending too much time holed up in the office lately. It was time to embrace new experiences and strike out in bold new directions.

Even if they were a little scary.

Since his was almost the last boat in the whole marina, they were soon leaving the club behind and heading out into the flat gray expanse of Houston bay.

Alicia's nerves tingled as they went farther and farther away from dry land. She couldn't see the opposite shore, so they seemed to be heading out into the wild blue yonder.

Rick pulled two frost-covered bottles of lager out of thin air.

"Refreshments." He grinned and flipped the tops off with a bottle opener. The glass felt cool and wet against her rather sweaty palm. "To adventure."

Alicia raised her bottle and clinked it against his. "And new experiences."

He took a sip, then leaned close. "Especially those of a sensual kind." His breath warmed her neck and made her shiver with pleasure. Their lips joined in a kiss that sent energy sparking through her.

"What are we doing?" she gasped, breaking the kiss. "We might get sucked out to sea."

"Anything could happen." Rick cocked his head. "And you might find you like it."

"You're such a tease." She sipped her chilled lager.

"What makes you think I'm teasing? Have I steered you wrong yet?" He nodded to his strong hand that guided the boat with the tiller.

"Well, no." A smile tugged at her lips. "I've been having a fantastic time with you."

"So you should be starting to trust me by now." Something flickered in the blue depths of his eyes. "At least a little bit."

"I apparently trust you enough to go out in a boat with you, so who knows what's next?" She looked about her, taking in the varied horizons—both industrial and pastoral—of Houston bay. "Tell me, can you get in your boat and go literally anywhere?"

"You mean, to the Bahamas, or Mexico?"

She nodded.

"Absolutely. All you need is enough water to drink and some food for the journey. No gas required." He grinned. "But it helps to know where you're going to dock. You usually can't just pull up on a beach unless it's a deserted island."

"Oooh. I like the sound of a deserted island. Nothing but palm trees, a crystal-clear lagoon…" She cocked her head. "And maybe an undiscovered tribe with a complex and interesting culture to explore."

"Always working, I see."

She shrugged. "What can I say? I love my work. And I tend to get on well with people so hopefully I could persuade them not to shrink our heads."

Rick guffawed. "I suspect traveling with you would be a real adventure."

"You should try it sometime."

"I think I am." His blue gaze rested on her face and she felt a wave of energy flow between them. "And so far I like it very much."

Alicia's heart squeezed. The time she'd spent with Rick could already be counted among the best hours of her life.

Was it possible that he felt the same way?

Could there be a real future between them?

As if in answer to her question, he took her hand in his. Their palms pressed together, their fingers wound into each other.

Rick turned to stare out over the prow. "I've spent a lot of my life chasing adventure. Always thinking that happiness was on top of the mountain, or just past the rapids, or around the next bend."

He turned back to her and met her eyes. "I think I've been looking in all the wrong places."

Alicia swallowed. She could almost hear the blood thundering in her veins as they sat, entwined, heading out into the unfamiliar wind and water of the bay.

What a dramatic turn her life had taken in the past week.

The fire seemed almost inconsequential compared to the seismic shifts in her inner and outer landscape.

Overnight—literally—she'd gone from being a "good little girl" plodding through her uneventful existence to being a sensual woman taking life by the horns.

Or by the tiller. "Can I have a turn steering?"

"Of course." His grin revealed that he loved her take-charge attitude. "Come sit up here and take over."

She eased herself into position and grasped the long, white handle that extended down into the belly of the boat.

She was surprised to find she had to work quite hard just to keep it steady. A quick jog to one side made Rick chuckle.

"The more you move it around, the slower you go."

"So, I guess you need strapping muscles to go fast enough for a race."

"Doesn't hurt, but it all comes with practice. Including the muscle."

Alicia's biceps muscle was beginning to feel like it might burst into flame, but she held the tiller steady as the boat plowed in a straight line through the steely water. "Wow. I like this."

She felt Rick's gaze on her face, and became aware of her chin tilted in pride and enjoyment.

"I like you liking it."

He pulled on a rope and did something with the sail that turned it slightly. The yacht moved faster over the water.

The wind whipped her hair behind her head and plastered her dress to her body.

"I feel like I'm flying!" Her words were almost lost in the wind.

"Yeah." Rick grinned. "Isn't it great? And flying's not so bad, either. I have a light aircraft I fool around in, too."

Alicia laughed. "Is there anything you haven't tried?"

Rick met her gaze with those soulful blue eyes. "Yeah. A lot of things. Some of them I never thought I'd want to try."

Like marriage.

And children.

The words flew past her, unspoken, but communicated as loudly as if he'd shouted them into the wind.

Alicia blinked, her chest tight. Maybe she was just imagining this whole relationship in her head. She really shouldn't get carried away. He was her first, but she certainly wasn't his.

Not even close.

So what made her think she'd be his last?

Rick moved close to her. He slid his arm around her waist while she did her best to hold their course steady. "You're going to make me wobble," she protested, as he leaned in to nibble her ear.

"A little wobbling might be interesting." He peered mischievously down the front of her life vest. "See if you can hang a left. There's a nice open spit of land on the far side of the bay."

Alicia pulled the tiller to the left, only to find the boat jag sharply to the right.

"Oops. Forgot to tell you that you turn it whichever way you don't want to go. Tiller Toward Trouble. So, if you're running from Jaws, you point the tiller at him and you'll take off in the opposite direction.

"I should point the tiller toward you," she teased, wrestling with the handle.

"Quite possibly. But I'd just chase faster." He shot her a wicked grin.

Alicia was both exhausted and exhilarated when they arrived back at the marina. She was also drenched with sea spray and cautious exploration confirmed that her hair was wild as Medusa's. "I must look a fright," she murmured, trying to catch her reflection in a shiny metal plate on the ship's deck.

"You look ravishing. In fact, I'm tempted to ravish you right now."

Rick's dark hair was tousled and shiny from the wind and spray. His eyes shone with excitement that mirrored her own.

"I'm tempted to ravish you right back," she whispered, casting a surreptitious glance at the grand clubhouse. "But I suspect we should wait until we're somewhere more private."

As they drew closer, she saw a crowd had gathered on the elegant balcony that faced the bay. "They're having some kind of party."

"There's always a party going on here. Those poor

people must not have decent homes to go to." He shook his head with pity. "I prefer a more *private* party."

The flash of heat in his eyes caused a rush of warmth between her legs.

"I think it's a barbecue."

No one looked that dressed up. She saw the two preppy guys in polo shirts and cargo shorts that they'd passed on their way out to the boat.

"They have them every Saturday."

"Looks kind of fun." She was still new to this life-styles-of-the-rich-and-famous thing, and sometimes it was a blast just to see a new place and meet some new people.

Again she noticed a strange flicker of darkness in Rick's eyes.

Then his usual teasing expression returned. "I'm afraid I'm not willing to share you with anyone right now." He growled slightly, so that only she could hear. "I've managed to keep my hands off that gorgeous body all afternoon and I can't wait a moment longer."

His hands left the tiller and appeared to move toward her of their own accord, which made the boat stray off their careful course into the marina.

"Watch out!" she called, grabbing the handle, as they drifted dangerously close to a gleaming monstrosity with yellow sails. "It's probably not hard to do a million dollar's worth of damage around here."

"Too right." He grinned, suddenly back under control, and steered *Titan III* into the forest of shiny masts with their colorful sails furled. "Glad I have you here to keep me on track. How did you like your first time out on the water?"

"I loved it."

Energy still danced through her, sparked by the exhilarating experience of steering the fast craft through the open water, harnessing the power of the wind.

"Then you'll come out again?" He raised a brow.

"I'd like to."

She'd more than like to, and not just because she'd discovered the fun of sailing. She wanted to spend more time with Rick. It was a relief to know that he already wanted to make plans beyond this weekend.

"Fantastic. I think next time we'll sail right out of the bay, into the gulf. What do you think?"

Anticipation trickled through her. "I think I'm ready."

Right now she felt ready for anything. Her quiet, humdrum existence of going to work and spending evenings with Alex seemed a distant memory.

Rick lashed the boat to the dock and helped Alicia back onto dry land.

"Oooh, I feel a bit wobbly," she gasped, as she attempted to keep her balance on the unmoving wood of the dock.

"That's what happens once you get your sea legs. It feels downright unnatural to stand on solid ground."

He moved close to her and slid his arms around her waist. He smelled heavenly: salt and sea air, mingling with his warm male scent.

Their lips met in a steamy kiss, and her hands slid around his waist to enjoy the muscles of his back through his rumpled cotton shirt.

When they pulled apart, she was breathless and wobbly. "I'm not sure that helped."

"Sorry." Rick shrugged and winked. "I guess we'd better get you home so you can recover in bed."

The flash of desire in his eyes suggested she would not be recuperating alone.

Heat crept through her. Then she hesitated. "I don't know. Maybe I should go back to the ranch and see what's going on."

"No way." Hands on hips, Rick made a show of barring her way. "The only place you're going is the penthouse suite of the Omni. Any other plans will have to wait."

Before she had a chance to protest, he slid one arm around her waist and the other behind her legs and swept her off her feet.

Alicia shrieked as he lifted her into the air. "You can't carry me!"

"Just watch me." He marched along the dock, a grin creasing his handsome face.

"I'm not that wobbly. I can walk, really." She tried to wriggle free, but she only rubbed against his hard chest, which made her pulse quicken.

"You give your sea legs a rest. You'll need your strength." His smile revealed even, white teeth. "Trust me."

Seven

The tray of fruit from room service was a work of art. Sliced peaches, plump berries, lush slabs of pineapple…but Alicia had no appetite for food.

"Champagne?" Rick popped the cork without waiting for her reply.

"Sure." She tried to sound calm, though her eyes were probably wide as saucers.

They'd showered—separately—and while she'd donned a soft, silk robe after drying off, Rick had marched into the living room wearing…nothing at all.

His body was tanned a deep nut brown from the waist up. Clearly he devoted ample time to leisure rather than sitting hunched over a desk all day.

His legs were paler, but sturdy and muscled. A spreading line of dark hair accentuated the ripped muscles of his chest as he held out the glass.

Alicia took it, trying not to stare.

"One of us is overdressed," he murmured, as he poured a second glass.

His dark hair curled, still damp, over his forehead, hanging almost to his piercing blue eyes.

"*Moi?*" she managed, taking a sip of champagne.

She'd never thought of herself as especially self-conscious about her body, but the idea of stripping off her robe—it was still broad daylight, after all—made her belly clench.

"*Toi.*"

"You speak French." Another surprise.

"Of course, I…" He hesitated, and a shadow passed over his brow. "I learned it in school."

He turned and walked across the living room, then pulled down the shade. They were so high up that no one could possibly see in, except perhaps from a helicopter, but she was touched that he considered her modesty.

The champagne sparkled over her tongue and the sight of his toned body heated her insides. While his back was turned, she undid the knot at her waist and slipped the robe down over her shoulders.

He walked to a second window and pulled the blinds. "Alicia, I have something to tell you—"

He turned, then stopped and stared, openmouthed. "Oh, Lord."

She'd let her robe fall to the floor and stretched out on the chaise like a Victorian courtesan. "Yes?"

"I…I…" His voice was a husky groan. "I can't seem to form a sentence."

"Then don't." She lifted a finger and beckoned.

Rick's chest rose as he inhaled deeply and walked across the floor, champagne glass in hand.

He knelt on the floor next to the chaise, and feasted on her with his eyes.

"The only reason people look at art is because they don't have a view like this to admire." His words caressed her ears as his hungry gaze heated her skin.

She writhed a little, exploring her newfound sensuality.

He didn't even have to touch her. Just being close to him made her insides shimmy and dampened her private, female places.

Her breathing quickened as he leaned closer. "You drive me crazy," he whispered into her neck.

"It must be my razor-sharp intellect," she teased. His intense arousal was shockingly visible—and only heightened her own fierce desire.

"Yeah, that, too." His eyes roamed over her breasts and belly, and along the length of her thighs.

Under his admiring gaze she felt deliciously sensual—beautiful—seeing herself for the first time through another's eyes.

The ordinary body that got her from A to B and stayed mercifully healthy and strong regardless of how many late nights she worked, had suddenly transformed into a garden of pleasure that begged to be explored.

Rick reached out his fingers slowly, as if afraid they might get burned. He held them above her waist, so close that she could feel his heat.

She lifted herself a fraction until her skin met his palm. His eyelids slid closed and he let out a sigh.

Then his hand started to roam. Over her hip and

along the full curve of her thigh. A seductive smile played on his lips as he slid an inquisitive finger in between her legs. "It's hot in there," he whispered.

"Burning hot," she breathed, as her hips jolted under his touch.

"I'd better do something about that." He lowered his head. "We don't want to set off the smoke alarms."

He pressed his wet mouth to her hot flesh and sucked.

Alicia's back arched and she moaned as sensation snapped through her. She reached for him, threading her fingers into his thick, damp hair and writhing under his mouth.

Already, the tension built inside her and she got that heavy, throbbing feeling that she was almost ready to explode. "Wait!" she cried. "Stop."

Rick stopped, eyes open and glowing.

"It's my turn."

A smile tilted the corner of his mouth when Alicia slid out of her prone position and pushed him gently down on the chaise.

She inhaled deeply and took his hard length in her hand. His erection throbbed, alive and sensitive, as she lowered her lips over its tip and savored a man for the first time.

Salty and silky, the taste only fueled her raging appetites. She took him into her mouth and sucked, enjoying the low groan that told her he loved this every bit as much as she was. She wrapped a hand around the shaft and caressed it while she licked the tip.

He touched her breasts—careful and cautious as a curator—while she explored and enjoyed his arousal.

When she couldn't stand the spiraling increase of tension, she slowly pulled her mouth back. "I'd like to go on top," she whispered, blushing.

"I'd love that." Rick's throaty enthusiasm gave her the encouragement she needed. Didn't he always? She was so lucky to have found a man she could trust with her embarrassing innocence.

They rolled on the condom together, then she climbed over him on the wide chaise and took him—slow and careful—into her hot, moist depths.

"Oh, my," she heard herself moan, as his hard length stroked ultra-sensitive nerve endings deep inside her. "I think I found the G-spot again."

Rick's chest shook in a silent laugh as she moved just enough to spark sensation that made her gasp. Somehow the feelings were even more intense and overwhelming in this position. Every move she made sent shockwaves of pleasure shooting through her.

She lifted her hips and slid back and forth, glad that she didn't have to pretend to be knowledgeable or cool or even capable—that she could enjoy the brand-new experience with the wide-eyed excitement she felt.

She discovered that if she kept him deep inside her, but rocked back and forth slightly, the sensations spread right though her crotch and up into her belly in a flush of pleasure. "Oh, my," she said again, conscious of her naive delight.

"I think you've found your clitoris," rasped Rick, his eyes squeezed shut as she writhed over him.

"Really?" A smile spread across her lips. "I can see why they make such a fuss over it."

Throbbing and pulsing seemed to have taken hold of

her down there, and she stopped thinking and gave herself over to the primal enjoyment flooding her mind and body.

She moved her hips in rhythmic motion until Rick's hands on her waist increased the speed and intensity and they reached an explosive and noisy climax together.

Alicia collapsed onto him, damp with perspiration and gasping like she'd just run a race.

Rick held her in his arms and stroked her hair. "You're amazing, wonderful, beautiful, sexy, brilliant and totally hot," he breathed, his chest heaving against hers.

Something leapt inside her. His words sounded so…heartfelt. Not like flattery or a meaningless compliment.

Rick Jones made her feel desirable and appreciated.

"You, too," she said with a grin. "And I'm so glad we're making up for all my wasted time."

"It's my pleasure." His words tickled her ear. "More pleasure than you can imagine."

She laughed and wriggled against him. "Well, since you've been gracious enough to initiate me into the delights of my own sensuality, I'd like to do something for you."

"I think you just did," he whispered, stroking her cheek.

"Something more…traditional."

"I'm not sure there's anything more traditional than sex. None of us would be here without it."

Alicia opened her eyes and met his humorous blue gaze. "You're so right, but none of us would be here without food, either. I'm going to cook for you."

"You don't have to do that."

"I know, I want to. I *love* to cook." She growled the words against his cheek. "It's a bit of a passion for me."

"You certainly are a woman of passion." He nipped at her neck.

A ripple of pleasure filled her. It was true! She actually was a woman of passion—after all these years of waiting to experience simple pleasures most people took for granted.

What a thrill—not to mention a relief—to find that she was as capable of passion as anyone on the planet.

"Cooking was probably my first love. Unlike other things, I learned it at a very young age and I've been practicing for a long time."

Rick shifted positions until they lay on their sides, facing each other. "The suite does have a kitchen…somewhere. It might be behind one of the doors at the end of the hallway. I never go down there."

Alicia mock-slapped his biceps. "You're terrible! You really never cook at all?"

"I'm ashamed to say I never do." He lowered dark lashes and pretended to look sheepish. "I'm totally dependent on room service for basic survival."

"Poor baby." She shook her head. "Because, let me tell you, a five-star chef has nothing on home cooking that's been made with love."

Rick's eyes widened slightly.

Alicia gulped.

Did she have to say the word *love* like that?

It was one thing saying she loved to cook, quite another to say she'd cook for him *with love*.

"I cook for all my friends," she stammered. "I love hosting dinners."

In other words, it doesn't really mean much at all.

Which wasn't true.

Rick had opened up something inside her, unlocked some hidden place she didn't know even existed. Maybe it was just sex—or passion—and all the new feelings they created in her, but she felt far more for him than she could express in mere words.

"I'm honored to be counted among your friends."

She blushed, sure he could see right through her.

His placid demeanor didn't hint at his emotions. Was he trying to tell her he just wanted to be friends? Or that any embarrassing slips of the tongue on the subject of *love* would be daintily glossed over?

Her chest grew tight. "What's your favorite kind of food?" Her voice sounded a little too high.

"I suspect it's your favorite thing to cook, whatever that is."

"Then let me surprise you."

Justin looked down to find his plate totally empty, just like the serving dishes of green and red curry, and the sticky rice noodles Alicia had served with them.

All that remained of the meal was the basil garnish and a satisfied feeling in his stomach.

"You're a goddess."

Alicia flushed. "It's nothing."

"Hardly. And you did surprise me. I wouldn't have expected Thai food."

"You thought I'd make something Mexican." She lifted a brow.

"You see right through me. I should have known you could never be predictable."

"I make some killer Mexican dishes, too." She smiled and crossed her arms. The topaz he'd given her sparkled at the top of seductive cleavage nestled in a silvery-white blouse.

Alicia Montoya literally glowed with confidence and sensuality. Everything about her was perfect.

And she'd just made what was hands down the very best meal he'd ever eaten.

"It's the fresh chilies." She leaned forward. "That's what makes both Thai and Mexican food really sing. One of these days I'm going to grow them myself. Maybe when I finally get my own place."

"What keeps you from moving out right now?"

"Alex."

"I'm sure he'd survive without you."

"One day he'll have to." A shadow passed over her brow. "At least I hope he will. I don't want to live with my brother for the rest of my life."

Maybe you could come live with me. The words hovered somewhere behind his teeth, until he grabbed a glass of dry white wine and washed them down his throat.

What was he thinking? He'd never asked any woman to live with him. He didn't even want male roommates, which was one of the reasons he lived all by himself in a huge hotel suite.

He liked his space. His freedom.

Didn't he?

Alicia rose and took both their plates. He grabbed them from her hands. "Let me take those." His voice came out a bit gruffer than he'd intended. "You've done enough."

"Oh, don't be silly. What are you going to do with them?" Her eyes sparkled. "You probably don't even know how to run the dishwasher."

"I could learn."

Alicia laughed. Still, he insisted on carrying the plates into the kitchen.

There were a lot of things he could learn. How to cherish the woman who brought a ray of bright, warm light into his life and heart. How to sustain a relationship beyond a month—something he'd never really wanted to do before. Heck, maybe he could even learn how to cook if those wicked hot chilies were involved.

He could even figure out how to have a very different relationship than his parents. And be a real father to his own children.

Children? Now he was truly getting ahead of himself.

He let his eyes drift to Alicia's lush, black-velvet-covered backside as she strode down the hallway just ahead of him, carrying the serving dishes.

Beautiful. And hot.

But so much more. Alicia had clearly obtained great pleasure from making this meal especially for him. She'd put thought and effort into every detail of the preparation and presentation. She'd made a simple dinner truly special.

This was the kind of woman he could imagine sharing all kinds of new experiences with. Maybe even sharing a life with.

His chest constricted. *One step at a time, Justin Dupree. First you need to tell her your real name.*

"Where are you going on your trip?" She turned to confront him with a bright, trusting smile.

"Hong Kong. Meeting with some dock officials."

"Sounds like fun." She entered the small but well-equipped kitchen where she'd made her magic.

"You should come." He meant it.

She laughed. "I have to work, remember? Even though my job doesn't pay megabucks, it means a lot to me. And I have people counting on me."

"Of course. I'll be back on Friday. We could spend next weekend together."

She didn't turn, but he saw her cheek lift in a smile, a smile that spread across the room to him.

Okay. He'd tell her next weekend.

He didn't want to spoil their perfect time together tonight and leave her with a bad taste in her mouth. Next Friday night he'd invite her over, give her something special from Hong Kong to sweep her off her feet, then 'fess up about his little white lie.

Yes. Much better.

He put the dishes into the dishwasher. "See, you can teach an old hound dog new tricks." He grinned, then slid his arms around her waist. "Now, where were we?"

Alicia had noticed a familiar car in the driveway, so she wasn't surprised to see a familiar face in the kitchen of El Diablo when she let herself in.

"Hi, Darius." She shook his hand.

"Hi, Darius?" Alex cut in. "You go away for the weekend and forget about your own brother?"

He walked toward her, his broad grin belying his accusation, and gave her a big bear hug. "I missed you like crazy, 'Manita, but I survived, see?"

"I do see." She kissed his cheek. "How are things going? Do the police have any leads?"

"Nope. That's why Darius is here."

Alicia knew him as another of the Texas Cattleman's

Club's newest members, the owner of a prominent security firm. The tall, dark-skinned man projected an air of effortless confidence. She also knew him as one of Lance Brody's best friends.

"He's looking into all the angles to see if we can figure out what's going on."

"And to make sure it doesn't happen again." Darius had a laptop open on the large island in the center of the kitchen. "Right now it looks like someone out there wants to frame Alex."

"But didn't they find gas cans?"

"Yep. Mine," said Alex. "From the tractor shed. I hadn't used them in months, so someone took them out and filled them, then brought them back here and set the fire."

"That's insane. Who could have done it?"

"No idea." Alex shrugged. "We don't lock the gates here, so anyone can come in and out."

"Anyone *could have* come in and out," corrected Darius. "We're going to put in a security camera and a keypad at the gate so that everyone will have to enter a code to come in and all activity will be recorded."

"I feel like a prisoner in my own home," growled Alex.

"It's for your own safety. And Alicia's." Darius typed on the keyboard. "We're going to set up a security camera near the barn, too."

"You can't be too careful," said Alicia with a shiver. A total stranger had stolen onto the ranch to wreak havoc and cast suspicion on Alex. "Do they still think you set the Brody fire?"

"They do. Lance Brody told Darius that someone saw my truck at the scene."

Alicia looked at Darius, who said nothing.

"That's ridiculous. There must be hundreds of trucks like yours in the Houston area," she said.

"I know. But if someone wants to believe I'm an arsonist, they'll trump up phony evidence any way they can."

"Why would anyone want to frame you?" Fear curled in her chest at the idea that someone would want to get Alex in trouble.

"There are plenty of people around here who'd be glad to see the back of me. Some folks are just bent out of shape that a kid from the barrio can own one of Somerset's finest ranches and become a member of the prestigious Texas Cattleman's Club."

"I admit we still have no leads," said Darius. He closed his laptop and looked up. "But we'll find the culprits of both fires and make sure they're convicted of their crimes."

"And I have faith that you'll find the truth."

Darius extended his hand, and after the slightest of pauses, Alex shook it.

Once the door had closed behind Darius, Alex strode back into the room.

"Alex, I'm surprised you'd have Darius Franklin do this, given how close he is to Lance Brody."

Alex shrugged. "He's the best man for the job, even if he doesn't choose his friends wisely. I trust him." He leaned in close to Alicia. "You look...different."

Alicia's face heated. "What? How on earth would I look different?"

"You're...glowing. Or something. I don't know. It's strange."

"I got a lot of sleep while I was there." Alicia blushed at her lie.

"Nice necklace." His dark eyes fixed on the topaz glittering at her neck.

Alicia's hand flew to it. "Thanks. Julie's Gems." She hoped he'd assume she'd bought it for herself.

"Pretty."

"I missed you."

"I missed you, too, 'Manita. I'm glad it's safe for you to come home. With Darius on the case, I feel we're close to finding out who did this."

"And why. That's the weirdest part."

"Human motivation is a strange thing. You think you know someone, then…" He threw his hands up in the air. "Be careful who you trust, that's what I always say."

He picked up an apple from the large fruit bowl in the center of the island and took a bite. "At least we can always count on each other."

"Absolutely." She uttered the word with conviction, while guilt and anxiety roiled in her stomach.

What would Alex say if he knew she'd spent the weekend with a man?

She longed to talk about Rick—she was overflowing with joy and excitement and hopeful anticipation. But better not to tell Alex, especially right now when he was so suspicious of everyone and everything.

She'd better go spill her guts to a girlfriend instead.

The airy indoor-outdoor café at the Texas Cattleman's Club bustled with a lunchtime crowd. Alicia was pretty sure she could air her confidences without being overheard.

And she sizzled with anticipation at the prospect.

Since joining the club, she'd grown close to Cara Pettigrew-Novak. They were friends years earlier while Cara's marriage to her college-sweetheart husband, Kevin, had slowly fallen apart, and she'd been thrilled to see them recently mend their broken bridges and get back together—apparently happier than ever.

She waved from her table as she caught sight of the statuesque blonde in the doorway. Cara waved back and weaved through the elegantly set tables toward Alicia.

They rose to kiss. "Oh, my goodness, you're positively radioactive," exclaimed Cara. She tucked her curly blond hair behind her shoulders and sank into her seat. "I can't wait to hear about the man who put that gleam in your eyes."

Alicia let out a wistful sigh, unable to stop a goofy grin from creeping over her face. "He's amazing."

Cara poured them both a glass of sparkling water. "I can tell, without you even saying a word. More details please!"

Alicia glanced around as if Rick might walk in at any moment and hear her bragging about him.

"Well, you remember the night I met him, when you were here at the club for Lance and Kate's reception. We just spent the most amazing weekend together," Alicia said.

"What does he look like?" Cara raised a slim, blond brow.

"Oh, tall, dark, handsome. Nothing special." Alicia blushed a little.

"Sure." Cara winked. "And I bet he doesn't have a muscle on his whole body."

"He is rather nicely built, even by your standards." Cara owned a chain of dance studios and always looked ready to compete in the Olympics. "Not to put too fine a point on it, he's perfect." Alicia sipped her water and the bubbles sparkled over her tongue.

"Oh, I'm not sure any man's perfect."

"Come on, you got back together with Kevin after all those years apart."

"Kevin certainly isn't perfect. He's pretty damn wonderful, though." A smile spread across her lovely face. "And I still love him like crazy."

"I know. I admit I used to be horribly jealous of you two. You were so lucky to meet the right man in college."

"Uh, hello? I almost divorced him. We've spent more time apart than we have together over the past few years. And part of the problem was that we found each other too early on. He wasn't ready to settle down, not really."

"I guess you're right. Good things come to those who wait."

"Something I've never been very good at, unfortunately." Cara waved to the waiter. "Why waste time reading the menu? Let's just have a hunk tell us what's good."

Alicia had noticed that the waiters at the Texas Cattleman's Club tended to be dashingly handsome. Their long white aprons gave the place an air of a refined European bistro.

A gorgeous young man with cropped dark hair approached the table.

"Could you tell us what's really sensational today?" asked Cara with an innocent smile.

"The red snapper is so fresh it's almost swimming. And the sauce made the chef cry. It's served on a bed of locally grown organic vegetables."

"Sold." Cara slapped her menu closed.

"Oooh. Me, too. And a Diet Coke."

"No wine?" Cara raised a brow. "I'll have a glass of pinot noir."

After the waiter had disappeared, she leaned toward Alicia. "I can't believe you're going to drink soda with a meal like this."

"I don't like to drink at lunch. Makes me tipsy."

"As long as there are no *other* reasons..." Cara narrowed her eyes.

Alicia gasped. "Absolutely not." She raised her hand in a three-fingered brownie salute. "On my honor." Then she paused as a chill swept over her. "At least I hope not."

"Please tell me you've been taking precautions."

"Yes. Of course I have."

It was time for her to get serious about contraception. Maybe take the pill or something. She'd never even needed to think about it before. Although they'd used condoms, she knew they weren't all that reliable.

"You don't sound too sure."

"Can we change the subject?" Alicia squeaked, as a flush crept up her neck.

"No way. Not until you tell me more about the man who has you glowing like a nuclear accident. Tell me his name again? I can't remember it."

"Rick Jones."

"Jones?" She pursed her pretty mouth. "I don't think I know anyone with that name. Which is funny, when you think about it. I guess he's not a member."

"I don't think so. I've mentioned his name a couple of times and no one seems to know him."

"How odd that you met him here, then. I suppose he must have been here as a guest. What does he do?"

"Something in shipping. He's in Hong Kong right now on business."

"There's big money in shipping."

"I kind of got that impression. He lives in a hotel suite."

She laughed. "That's one way to avoid cleaning and cooking."

"Yes. He's totally unembarrassed about his inability to do either."

"I guess he saves his energy for other pursuits." Cara lifted a brow.

Alicia felt her face heat up. "You're absolutely right. And he sails, too. We went out on his yacht."

"A yacht!" Cara clapped her hands together. "I love it. Was it one of those huge things with a full-size kitchen and a staff of ten?"

"No, a slick racing yacht with barely room to turn around."

"Really?" Cara frowned and put down her fork. "Have you ever met Justin Dupree?"

Alicia racked her brain. "Nope. Don't think so."

"He's a member so you'll run into him sooner or later. He's heir to some vast shipping empire. Absolutely rolling in it, or so they say. And he's into yacht racing, too."

"Weird. I guess those pursuits aren't all that unusual around here."

"Not if you're loaded to the gills." Cara rolled her

eyes. "I'm glad it's not him, though. He's a serious skirt chaser. I'd be giving you some stern warnings."

"Well, I honestly have no idea what Rick is like when I'm not with him. We've only spent time alone so I haven't actually met any of his friends." She sighed. "He's so gorgeous he must have women falling all over him."

"But he has eyes only for you."

"So far." Alicia smiled. "He's been unbelievable. I'm not very…experienced." She cleared her throat, unwilling to admit exactly how inexperienced she was. "And he's been so thoughtful and caring."

"He sounds like a keeper. Has he met Alex yet?"

Alicia stopped, her glass suspended in the air. "Not yet."

Cara laughed. "You're afraid, aren't you?"

"Of course not! Alex is perfectly reasonable."

"Oh, come on! He tried to stop you from seeing *me* when we were first friends. He thought I was fast or something, because I did a lot of dancing and cheerleading."

"He's very traditional." Why did she always feel such a strong urge to defend Alex?

"Traditional? He's downright Neanderthal when it comes to protecting you. Still, if you need a buffer there when you tell him about Rick, I'll be there for ya. We could even get together right here in the café. Nice and informal."

"I don't think so." Alicia winced. "I only just started dating him. I don't want to freak him out. Not yet, anyway." She giggled. "But if things continue the way they've been going so far, I may well take you up on your offer."

"I'm glad to hear it. You deserve to meet someone fabulous."

"I agree." Alicia raised her Diet Coke and clinked it against Cara's wineglass. "To romance."

The snapper smelled sensational when it arrived, borne by the equally delicious waiter.

She took a bite. "I can see why the chef cried. Then again, since I met Rick everything seems…brighter, richer, more flavorful. Is that crazy?"

"Absolutely. Sounds like love."

"Oh, it can't be love. Like I said, we only just met. We've had a few dates, and I spent one weekend with him."

"Sometimes that's all it takes. Where is his suite?"

"The Houston Omni, near the Galleria. It has views all over Houston—it's incredible."

Cara paused. "The Omni? I'm pretty sure that's where Justin Dupree lives. I went to a wild party there a couple of years ago. You could see all of downtown from his living room." Her friend's face turned serious. "Are you sure it's not him?"

Alicia shook her head, perplexed. "His name's Rick. Of course it's not him."

"I don't know, Alicia. He's a shipping heir, tall, dark and handsome, races yachts and lives at the Houston Omni. Don't you think that's a bit too much of a coincidence?"

Alicia frowned. "That is odd."

"I have a weird feeling it's the same guy."

Cold fear skated down Alicia's spine. "Why would he change his name?"

"I can't even begin to imagine." Cara frowned. "You

know what? There's a picture of Justin Dupree in last month's *Vanity Fair*. Let's go look at it and you can tell me if he looks anything like your Rick. They've probably still got a copy in the library."

Eight

The library's stone fireplace and gleaming black and white floor always gave Alicia the sense of being in a grand castle.

Today, she felt like she was heading for the execution block.

Couldn't Cara just let her enjoy her first-ever chance to brag about a hot date?

Now a creepy mystery cast a shadow over her glorious weekend with Rick.

Or at least she thought he was Rick.

Cara riffled through a stack of magazines spread over a low shelf while Alicia stood nearby.

Doubts skated around her mind, bumping into faith that it was all a silly misunderstanding. Hopefully Justin Dupree—whoever he was—would look nothing whatsoever like Rick.

"There he is." Cara stabbed the shiny page with a fingernail, then handed it to Alicia.

Her red snapper turned into a lead ball in her stomach when she saw the picture: Rick, gorgeous in black tie, with both arms wrapped around the impossibly slim waist of a smiling blonde in a barely-there dress.

She scanned the caption: "Shipping Heir Justin Dupree Squires Mila Jankovich to Blake Foundation Gala."

Her rib cage turned into a vice, tightening over her heart. "It's him," she breathed. "I can't believe it. Why would he lie to me?" Tears already hovered in her voice.

"I don't know, sweetie, but we'll find out." Cara slid an arm around her back.

Alicia's initial shock was quickly morphing into anger. "Why didn't he want me to know who he is? I noticed he didn't introduce me to anyone at the yacht club." She frowned and put the magazine down on a table. "And now that I think about it, he wouldn't come into this club with me, either. Now I know why." She blew out a breath. "It might have been awkward if one of his buddies slapped him on the back and said, 'Hey, Justin!'"

"It is odd. He's a member here, though he doesn't come all that often. I guess he travels a lot. Or maybe just hangs out at the yacht club, instead."

"You know him?"

"I've met him. He's friends with Mitch and Lance."

"Mitch and Lance *Brody?*" Alicia's eyes widened.

Cara smiled. "Do you know any other Mitch and Lance combos?"

Alicia's body grew cold. "Mitch and Lance think Alex set the fire at their refinery. They hate him."

A nasty possibility occurred to her. "Do you think

they could have sent Justin my way to dig up information about Alex?"

Cara stared at her, blue eyes wide with confusion. "I can't imagine they'd stoop to something like that. I admit I don't know Justin all that well, but I'm sure he's too busy to get involved in intrigues." She squeezed Alicia's hand. "Oh, sweetie, I know how much he meant to you."

"Believe me, I am eternally in your debt." Her voice sounded as calm and cold as she felt. "I'm glad I found out now and not after he'd had more fun at my expense."

"I'm pretty sure Kevin knows him. Maybe he can shed some light on the whole situation."

Humiliation burned in Alicia's gut. "Please don't tell Kevin. Or anyone." She glanced over her shoulder and was glad to find the library empty. "It'd be so awful if everyone knew. Or if Alex found out."

Ugh! She'd trusted her own instincts for once, followed her pathetic, girlish heart, and look what happened.

She blinked to keep tears from springing to her eyes.

"Hey, here's a crazy idea." Cara reached into her bag for a tissue and offered it, but Alicia shook her head. "Why don't you *ask* him?"

"Ask Rick? I mean, *Justin?*" She snorted. "I wouldn't even know how to address him when he picked up the phone." She shook her head. "I'd rather die than give him another chance to lie to me."

Her spine grew rigid as she realized the extent of his deception. "We spent the whole weekend together—literally every hour—so he had ample time to tell me who he really is if he was ever going to. Which apparently he wasn't."

"It doesn't make any sense."

"The only way it makes sense is if he wanted to keep me separate from his real life. A bit on the side." She glanced back at the glossy issue of *Vanity Fair.* "Why does that woman look familiar?"

"She's a model." Cara waved a hand as if to dismiss her. "Does some fashion stuff and a bunch of Revlon ads. Very overexposed."

"Great. His real girlfriend is a supermodel. I guess I should feel bad for her, too." The tears threatened again. "I want to go home."

"Listen, Alicia, that picture means nothing. Just because he took some girl to a gala does not mean he's engaged to her."

"Then why is he wrapped around her like a tortilla?" She shrugged her clutch bag higher under her arm. "It doesn't matter anyway. It's over between us."

"Oh, sweetie. Maybe there's some perfectly reasonable explanation."

"Yeah. Maybe he was abducted by aliens and they sent him back to earth with a new identity." She cocked her head.

"I said a *reasonable* explanation."

"When you come up with one, give me a call."

"I'm so sorry." Cara's pretty face was taut with distress. "I wish I wasn't the bearer of the bad news."

Alicia gave her a hug. "You're a true friend. A lot of people would have let me go on seeing him because they didn't want to make waves. I'm very grateful. I just need to go home and have a good cry."

Justin couldn't understand it. He'd called Alicia when he landed in Hong Kong and left a message on her cell.

No response.

Okay, so some people had trouble with international dialing codes. He called back first thing the next morning, which was early evening in Houston.

No answer. Left another message.

Now, three days later he'd left at least six messages and had yet to hear a word from her.

He loosened his tie and stretched out in the leather chair at his hotel desk.

Not talking to her was driving him mad. If he couldn't enjoy the feel of her soft body against his, he at least wanted to hear her warm, sensual voice over the phone. He missed her with an ache that tightened his muscles. He couldn't remember ever hurting this badly for a woman.

Alicia was so different from all the other women he'd dated. Self-possessed and calm, she didn't try to impress him by bragging about her accomplishments. Instead, he had to tease them out of her.

She was thoughtful and caring, as evidenced by the lovely dinner she made for him. Ever since, he'd been longing to try his hand in the kitchen so he could make something for her and return the gesture.

In addition to being brilliant and kind, she was also smoking hot between the sheets—and anywhere else they happened to be when the mood struck.

And fun. Sailing with her had been a blast. He could tell her first taste of speed had given her an appetite for more. She'd be a great racing companion, with her no-nonsense, practical attitude and her sunny approach to life.

She was a great companion, period. And he wanted

to spend a lot of time with her. Possibly even the rest of his life.

Justin blew out hard. Suddenly everything looked different. Traveling wouldn't be an end in itself if he had Alicia to come home to. He wouldn't need to blow off steam by partying and jumping off mountains anymore.

He could think of far better ways to unwind—in Alicia's arms.

His phone lay on the desk, its shiny black surface an affront. He wanted to pick it up and call her again, but there was such a thing as coming on too strong.

Not something he'd ever thought about before.

Usually he was the one hoping someone would back off. He generally tired of women before they tired of him—right around the time they started hinting at something permanent.

That sent him off in a cloud of dust.

Justin frowned.

Maybe Alicia needed to cool off a little after all the time they'd spent together.

When he got back he'd bring her a big bunch of flowers, deal with the awkward business about his name, and start over again.

He leaned back in his chair. Only three more days. He could handle it.

"You've been working late all week." Alex frowned at Alicia as she came through the door at the ranch late on Friday evening. Her usual glow had noticeably dimmed and she seemed rushed and tense.

"Busy. We're gearing up for a visiting exhibition,

which involved stripping down the big gallery and packing all the pieces away. Today the walls went up, but they still need painting."

She marched into the kitchen and threw her big leather bag on the island. "And I've got a bunch of phone calls to make about the plans for downtown."

"No wonder you look tired." He crossed his arms over his chest. "But usually you love all that stuff. You hate having too little to do. Is something else going on?"

She blinked, and if he wasn't mistaken, she swallowed. "Nope. Nothing." She bustled over to the fridge and started unloading storage containers onto the island.

"Alicia...." He said her name in the singsong way that drove her crazy. "I don't believe you."

"Don't then." She opened up a container and sniffed.

Alex frowned. She hadn't actually snapped at him, but that's what it felt like.

Something was definitely going on. His first instinct was to collar his baby sister and make her 'fess up. But his urge to protect Alicia sometimes threatened to drive a wedge between them. He held himself in check. She was a grown woman, and entitled to some privacy.

He wasn't going to say a single word.

Not yet, anyway. If she was still moping by Monday he wouldn't be able to restrain himself.

The phone rang, and instead of moving to answer it like she usually did, Alicia started spooning leftover casserole into a baking dish.

"I'll get it," he said. She did too much around here. Who was he to assume it was her job to answer the phone, anyway?

"No." Her sharp answer made him stop in his tracks. "I will."

But instead of picking up the phone on the wall in the kitchen, she hurried down the hall to the den.

And she didn't pick it up there, either.

Alex stuck his head out the kitchen door in time to see her crouch to read the caller ID. Instead of picking up the handset, she pushed the button to send the message straight to voice mail.

Curiosity overtook him. Like a *vaquero* stealing up on a runaway calf, he crept down the hallway.

With her attention fixed on the machine blurting its greeting in her friendly voice, Alicia didn't even see him.

"Alicia, it's me…uh…Rick. I've been calling your cell all week but there's no answer. I know you told me not to call you at home, but I'm worried about you."

Cold shock settled into Alex's stomach.

Alicia was seeing someone. Or not seeing him. Apparently, she was avoiding this *Rick's* phone calls.

This man was bothering her. Pestering her.

Rick who? He didn't know any Rick. He was nervous about her being around those moneyed hotshots at the Texas Cattleman's Club, but so far she hadn't shown a peep of interest in any of them.

Or so he'd thought.

He sucked in a deep, silent breath. Alicia stood watching the phone, arms crossed and eyes narrowed.

"I don't know what's going on, but I had a wonderful time with you and I'm really looking forward to seeing you again. I'm back in Houston and you know where to find me. So, call me, okay?"

The machine clicked off. Something in Alex clicked into the *on* position. "Who the hell was that?"

Alicia wheeled around and gasped. "What are you doing listening to my phone calls?"

"Since when did you start keeping secrets from me?"

Tears welled in her big brown eyes. "Since I started wanting a life of my own." Anger and pain rang in her voice. "But I haven't been doing a very good job of it, so go ahead and yell at me."

She stormed past him down the hallway and back into the kitchen. She shoved the casserole dish into the microwave and punched the numbers with uncharacteristic drama.

Alex fought the urge to yell.

His natural instinct to go ballistic was an "opportunity," according to the corporate management book he'd been reading lately. An opportunity to become more...approachable.

He drew in a measured breath. "Would you like to tell me what's going on?"

"Not really." She swiped at a tear with her wrist, and turned to pull the lid off a container of day-old rice.

When Alicia stopped cooking and started reheating leftovers, something was very wrong.

"What did this Rick do to you?" He managed to keep his tone even.

"Nothing. Nothing at all. It doesn't matter." She slammed open a kitchen cabinet and retrieved two dishes with a loud clatter.

"Alicia Montoya, I know you better than I know myself and I don't think I've ever seen you this upset. Now you want to lie to me and tell me everything's okay?"

She stopped dead, hands frozen in midair with their plates.

"I don't want to lie to you, Alex." She turned, slowly, and set the plates on to the island. "I don't ever want to lie to you, or to anyone else."

She took a deep breath and tucked a strand of hair behind her ear. Then she lifted her chin and looked him dead in the eye with an expression he'd never seen before. "I spent last weekend with him."

A fist closed around Alex's heart. "At his house?"

"In a hotel."

Alex's lungs couldn't hold air. This sleazebag had taken his baby sister to a hotel? Probably some lowlife motel filled with hookers and junkies and... "Where can I find him?"

Alicia pursed her lips with distaste. "And you wonder why I didn't tell you about him?" She crossed her arms over her chest. "You treat me like a little kid. You *made* me sneak around. I would have liked to tell you about him and see if you know him and ask you what you think, but because you turn into a raging beast at the thought of me dating a mere mortal, I couldn't."

Alex frowned. Was this true?

She'd dated. He remembered those sorry losers who came to the house over the years.

He'd made sure to let them know that Alicia was not just any girl they could grope and fondle and tell their friends about. Maybe he had scared a few of them off.

"You deserve the best, 'Manita."

"I know you only want to protect me, but it's too much. I'm twenty-six and I need to make my own mistakes." Her stern demeanor wavered. "And I just made one, but it's okay. I learned from it, and I'll know what to do differently next time."

Alex worked hard to keep his breathing steady. The urge to pummel someone—namely this Rick—made his blood pump fast and hard. "I'm glad you learned from your mistake." Good. His voice sounded nice and calm.

"We went out a few times and I really liked him." Her eyes shone with pleasure. Which was like a fist of very unpleasant feeling to Alex's gut.

"He was sweet, considerate." Her expression hardened. "So, after the fire, I decided to go stay with him."

"You lied to me."

"I did. There was enough drama already. I didn't need to make more, for either of us. I just wanted to spend the weekend with a man I'd grown to like." A frown furrowed her pretty forehead. "But he turned out to be a totally different man altogether."

Adrenaline flashed through Alex. "Did he hurt you?"

"No! Nothing like that at all. But he's not right for me. That's all that matters." Her gaze implored him not to pry further.

He stepped forward and took her in his arms. She softened and let him hug her.

"You be careful with those rich boys at the club. Those kind of men eat girls like you for breakfast."

"I know. I wasn't planning to date one of them. It just happened. But it's over now. Can we leave it in the past?"

"Sure, 'Manita. Just one of those things."

Rick. The name didn't ring a bell. He'd put out feelers though. By this time tomorrow he'd know who'd made his baby sister cry. And then he'd figure out what to do with him.

* * *

Justin scanned the café at the Texas Cattleman's Club. No sign of Alicia. He poked his head in the game room. Still nothing. He was about to go explore the library, when a hand on his arm stopped him.

"Justin Dupree, I presume." Cara Pettigrew-Novak fixed him with a steel-blue gaze.

"At your service, ma'am."

"Just checking, because I thought you might be someone called Rick Jones."

Justin frowned. "I've been known to use that alias on occasion." He arched his brow.

"So I hear. You used it on my friend Alicia."

"Where is Alicia? Is she okay?" Urgency sparked through him.

"She's fine, no thanks to you. Why did you give her a fake name?"

Was that why she wouldn't return his calls? He knew she wouldn't like it, but he was pretty sure it wouldn't be a deal breaker. Not after they'd shared so much together.

"I use it all the time. Keeps the press off my trail."

"Alicia isn't a journalist."

"I know that, now."

"Did you ever think she was?" Cara tilted her chin.

"No. I didn't." He narrowed his eyes. "What exactly is going on? Does Alicia know I'm Justin Dupree?"

"She does."

"How?"

"I told her." She crossed her arms. "I thought she should know. Don't you?"

"Yes, of course. I was planning to tell her." Why was

he having this conversation with Cara, when he should be talking to Alicia? "Is she here?"

"Nope. Haven't seen her. I hear someone broke her heart."

Justin gulped. "She was upset?"

"Really, really upset."

"Damn." His chest tightened. "I've got to explain."

"That you didn't want the press on your trail?" She chuckled. "I'm not sure that will go over well."

"That I wanted to tell her because I…because she…" *Because I've never met anyone I care about so much.* "Where is she?"

"At home, I imagine. El Diablo." She leaned close. "It was cruel, you know, giving her a fake name so she wouldn't know she was being seduced into bed by one of the foremost ladies' men in all Texas."

"Cara, you exaggerate." He tried to make light of her barb. "And I didn't seduce her. At least I don't think I did. It was mutual. And why am I telling this to you?"

"I told her she should give you a chance to tell your side of the story. I assured her there was probably a perfectly reasonable explanation. So far, I haven't heard one, but…" She shrugged her slim shoulders. "She didn't seem very interested."

"I've got to go see her." He reached into his pocket for his car key.

"You'll recall that she lives with her brother." Cara tilted her head, waiting for his reaction.

"Alex Montoya. I'm sure he'll be reasonable."

She laughed. "He can be, under the right circumstances—which these definitely aren't." She patted his arm. "Listen, I don't know you that well, but you seem like an okay guy. At least that's what Kevin, Lance and Mitch say."

"I'm honored."

"And Alicia was pretty smitten with you before I clued her in to your little deception. I hope you two manage to work it out."

"Me, too."

The gate to El Diablo was locked, and Justin had to use the intercom to request admittance.

"Name?"

He thought for a second. "Rick Jones." That's what she'd expect him to call himself.

With relief, he saw the gate swing open, and he drove in.

Cattle grazed in fenced pastures on either side of the long curving drive that led up to the grand old house. Alex Montoya had done well for himself—and for Alicia—especially considering their humble background.

Alex was a smart man. Hopefully not one to jump to rash conclusions, or hold a grudge.

Yeah. Right. He and Lance had one of the longest-running grudges in local history.

He parked in the turnaround in front of the house and stepped out. Before he'd reached the shady porch, Alex emerged from the front door, his dark, intense eyes set in a fierce glare.

His deep voice boomed through the air. "Since when do you go by the name Rick Jones?"

"Is Alicia at home? I need to speak with her, Alex."

"She doesn't want to see you." Alex took the steps two at a time, until he was standing chin to chin with

Justin. Alex's chin, however, was several inches higher than his. "You can leave now."

"I'd appreciate the chance to talk with her."

"That won't be possible." The taller man's eyes narrowed. "Do you always use a fake name with women that you plan to use and cast aside? Nice girls who don't have blue blood so they're ripe for the plucking?"

Alex's eyes flashed. He grabbed Justin by the shirt, knuckles digging into his chest.

"It's a bit more innocent than that. I get hounded by the paparazzi so sometimes I resort to—"

"If you didn't sleep with so many damned heiresses, the paparazzi wouldn't be interested in you," Alex hissed right in his face. "If you come near my sister again, I'll, I'll… I don't know what I'll do, but let's not find out."

He removed his fist from the front of Justin's shirt and looked at it as if it had a mind of its own.

"Your sister means a lot to me." He held his head high. "She's a very special person."

"You think I don't know that?" Alex cocked his head and stared hard at Justin. "My sister is too good for someone who associates himself with the Brody brothers." His voice took on a tone of polished steel.

"Mitch Brody and I have been good friends for a long time, and I know his brother Lance, too. They're good men, Alex."

Alex leaned in until Justin could smell the testosterone rolling off him. "Did they put you up to this?"

"Of course not. I happened to meet Alicia at the club, we struck up a conversation and became friends." Which was the truth. Justin had volunteered to get information on Alex for the Brodys; they hadn't asked him to. The thought of it now made him feel sick. How could he have even considered doing that to Alicia?

"Do I look like I was born yesterday?" Alex's hands looked like they were itching to wrap themselves around Justin's neck.

"Alicia is a beautiful and intelligent woman. I don't need an ulterior motive to be interested in her. As I've tried to explain, I care for her very much. The name thing was a misunderstanding. Entirely my fault. If you'd just let me speak to Alicia for a few minutes, I'm sure—"

"Get off my ranch!" Steam was about to start rising out of Alex's dark hair. "If you don't leave now, I'll have my men tow your car—and you—to the gates."

"Alex." Alicia appeared behind him in the doorway. "It's okay. I can handle it."

Justin's heart surged. "Alicia, I can explain."

"Go back inside, 'Manita. He's leaving."

Alicia came down the steps in faded jeans that hugged her spectacular legs and a simple denim shirt. Ravishing. "Alex, I said I can handle it. I'm not a baby."

Her eyes met Justin's and energy crashed between them. Hope swelled in his chest.

"I've been burning to tell you my real name, but the time never seemed quite right. I'm mortified that you found out and I promise to make it up to you."

Alicia strode past Alex, boot heels firm on the hard ground. "Get in your car. I'll ride to the gate with you."

"Maybe we could sit somewhere and talk."

Alicia ignored him, rounded his Porsche and opened the passenger side.

"'Manita, I don't think you should—" Alex's interjection was cut off by Alicia slamming the car door shut.

Justin turned his back on Alex and got in on the driver's side. He turned to look at her. "I missed you," he said softly.

"Start the engine." She stared straight ahead.

He hesitated for a second, then turned the key. "Cara told me what happened."

"Yes. I felt like a real ass."

"I'm so, so sorry. I never meant for you to find out from someone else."

He wasn't embarrassed by the pleading tone in his voice. Part of him was just grateful and relieved to be sharing a space with her again.

"Drive." She nodded to the gearshift. Justin reluctantly shifted into Drive and started along the driveway. "I don't want to see you again."

"Alicia, you don't mean that."

"Trust me—and me, you can trust, I'm pretty straightforward, unlike some people—so trust me, I mean it with every bone in my body."

"I use the name Rick Jones all the time. I'm registered at the hotel under that name."

"You registered with a fake license and credit card?" She cocked a brow.

"Well, no. They do know my real name, but officially, on the books, I'm Rick Jones."

"But they have the privilege of knowing your real name. A privilege I was not granted." Her voice was silvery and cool, not the warm caress he remembered. "Even after we slept together."

"I wanted to tell you since the beginning. I tried several times but…"

"But what?"

He shoved a hand through his hair. "I guess I knew all along that it would be a big deal to you. Once I got to know you, that is. I could tell that you'd consider even a minor fib to be a huge deception."

"You were right about that. And I'd hardly consider lying about your identity to be a minor fib."

Despite him driving as slowly as the car would go, they were dangerously close to the gates. Kidnapping her was tempting, but definitely not a good idea under the circumstances.

"What can I do to make it up to you?"

"You can't. As I said, I don't wish to see you again. Since we're both members of the Texas Cattleman's Club, there's no way we can avoid each other completely, but I see no reason for anything beyond a polite greeting in the future."

She held her head with the dignity of a queen. Strange how someone could look so regal when dressed like a cowgirl, but that was Alicia Montoya. A woman of many dimensions, each more fascinating and compelling than the last.

If he told her he loved her, would that melt her hardened heart?

He cursed the thought even as it occurred to him. If he told her right now she'd think he was toying with her.

"Could I take you out on my yacht again, as a friend?" He didn't try to cajole or sweet-talk her. She'd loved sailing though, he could tell.

"No. You can stop right outside the gates. I'll walk back in."

"Alicia, you're making too much of this."

"That's your opinion. As you've already admitted,

you knew it would be a big deal to me so you deliberately continued to conceal the truth. I told you all kinds of confidences."

She turned to look at him, finally, eyes filled with tears. "I told you about my childhood, and my family, and all our private hopes and dreams. And you chose to disrespect me by keeping the truth from me, so it wouldn't interfere with all the hot sex we were having."

A fat tear fell and rolled down one lovely cheek.

Justin's heart ached to bursting. He longed to reach out and touch her, but he knew that would propel her from the car.

"It wasn't just about sex." His voice was gruff. "You mean a lot more to me than that. I truly enjoyed every minute we spent together. I was afraid of spoiling it, yes. I figured the longer we spent together and the more you got to know me, the less of a big deal it would be when I finally told you. I almost gave it away when you noticed I spoke French—my family is originally from France and we've always spent enough time there to become fluent. I was about to turn and tell you everything, but there you lay, naked and resplendent, and the words withered on my tongue because I didn't want to drive you away."

A tear rolled down Alicia's other cheek. She did nothing to brush it away. "I trusted you. I came to you asking for help. You knew I was innocent—dangerously naive, even—and you took advantage of that. Why didn't you tell me you were friends with the men who are trying to frame my brother for arson? Or that you already knew my brother? How could you keep that from me?"

"I didn't think it—"

"I don't even want to know." She shook her head. "After what's happened between us I could never trust you again, and I don't intend to try."

"But—" Panic surged through Justin as she reached for the door handle.

"Please, don't come to El Diablo again. You won't be welcome here."

"I'll call you, after you've had some time to think."

"No. Don't call, don't visit, don't write." She turned a cold, dark gaze on him. "I'll be polite when I meet you in company, but don't for a single second think that it means I've forgiven you."

She swung her long denim-clad legs to the ground, then slammed the door.

It couldn't have hurt more if she'd slammed it right on his heart.

Nine

Justin heaved his clubs back into his locker. He'd whacked a ball around all eighteen holes of the Texas Cattleman's Club golf course, and it hadn't helped a bit. His muscles stung with energy and his legs itched to run.

He couldn't stand still, or sit, or sleep when every fiber of his body ached to be with Alicia.

"Hey, Justin!" Kevin Novak strode into the locker room, blond hair windblown, hauling his own clubs. "I hear you're in the doghouse with my wife."

"Yeah. The girls have closed ranks against me." He shut the locker door. "Can't say I blame 'em though. I'm guilty on all counts."

Kevin pulled out his driver and wiped off the end with a cloth. "I can see the advantages of having a double identity. You could get up to all kinds of tricks and no one could pin it on you." He winked. "Sounds fun."

"That's all in the past. I don't want to play tricks on anyone, but old habits die hard and all that. Rick Jones is dead. I killed him myself. I stand before you and everyone else as Justin Dupree."

"The only man crazy enough to pursue Alex Montoya's sister."

Justin walked over to Kevin. "Alicia is the most incredible woman I've ever met. I'd walk through fire for her."

"I'm sure her brother would be happy to arrange that." Kevin raised a brow.

"Yeah. Can't blame him though. If I had a sister I'd probably feel the same way."

"Do you think she'll ever forgive you?"

"She won't give me a chance to get close to her. She was here this morning and barely acknowledged me." He let out a long sigh. "I've closed billion-dollar deals with my archrivals in the business world, but I can't even get her to look my way."

"You need a plan." Kevin settled his humorous blue gaze on him. "And I think I have one. Why don't Cara and I invite you and Alicia to dinner? Then you'll be on neutral turf and you can talk things out."

"Alicia would never agree."

"She will if we don't tell her you'll be there."

"She'll leave when I show up."

"No, she won't. She and Cara are good friends, and Alicia's very polite and thoughtful. I don't think she'd blow off a dinner someone else spent time preparing."

"You might be onto something there. But will Cara go for the idea?"

Kevin put his clubs in his locker. "Cara's got a soft spot for you. She thinks you're ready to settle down and enjoy some wedded bliss."

"She does, huh?"

"Hey, I screwed things up between Cara and me because I wasn't ready for family life when we first got married. I put all my energy into making money and almost lost the truly important things no amount of money can buy. I've been given a second chance and I feel it's my duty to help another lonely man find the way to his woman's heart."

"Kevin Novak, a romantic. Now I've seen everything."

"I just know how good it feels to enjoy life with the woman you love."

"I hear you. I'd do almost anything to get back in Alicia's good graces."

"How about Saturday?" Kevin shut his locker.

"If you think this crazy idea will work, then I'm game."

A small knot formed in Alicia's stomach as she rode in the elevator up to Cara and Kevin's apartment in downtown Houston. She was eternally grateful to Cara for alerting her to Justin's deception, but how much had Cara told her husband? She'd begged Cara to keep the embarrassing truth secret, but married couples probably shared everything.

She'd always hoped to have a marriage with no secrets. Or even just a relationship.

Anger trickled through her when she thought about how Justin Dupree had duped her. He'd taken something from her—trust—and it would be a long time, if ever, before she got it back again.

"Alicia!" Cara greeted her with a kiss at the open door. "Come in, we're so pleased you could come."

"Alex didn't want to let me out of the house." Alicia gave Cara her jacket and walked into the chic, modern space. "He's hovering over me more than ever. I think he'd like to rip Justin Dupree limb from limb."

"Yikes." Cara made a face. "Still, I think it's adorable how protective he is."

"I wish he'd find someone else to protect." She sighed. "Though I can't say I blame him. Apparently, I need protecting."

"You do not. It was a silly misunderstanding. Justin's really sorry."

"And how do you know? You haven't talked to him, have you?"

"Well, actually—" Cara reddened. "Come in and have a drink."

"You didn't, did you?" Alicia grabbed her arm, panic surging inside her. The idea of people sitting around whispering about her humiliation made her want to curl up into a ball. "Please, tell me you didn't say anything."

"Sweetie," Cara squeezed her hand, "I know you want to forget about the whole thing, but I think that would be a terrible waste."

"What do you mean?" A bad feeling crept over her. "What are you up to?"

"Come into the living room." Cara tugged her by the hand. "I made my world-famous cheese puffs."

"You know I can't resist those." Alicia forced a smile to hide a growing sense of dread. "The apartment is lovely." She might as well attempt to be polite.

"Thanks. We're both counting the days until our house in Somerset is ready. They should break ground next month."

Cara pulled her through a double doorway into a large living room. Candlelight glowed on a low table in front of the inviting black sofa and classical music rose from hidden speakers.

"Hi, Alicia." A deep, familiar voice rose from somewhere as hidden as the speakers.

Alicia stopped dead, gripped by panic.

Justin came into view on the left side of the room, holding a tumbler. She tried to focus on his glass so she didn't have to meet the gaze of those intense blue eyes.

She gulped. "Cara, what's going on?"

"Kevin and I wanted to have a couple of our good friends to dinner." She tugged on Alicia's hand, but Alicia remained rooted to the spot. "White or red wine? Or would you prefer something else?"

I'll be polite when I meet you in company.

Could she follow through on her promise?

"Justin." She nodded. Then she swept past him. She did not take his offered hand or even look him full in the face. It was the best she could do for now.

Every fiber of her being screamed for her to run straight out the door, but what would that accomplish? This was the first day of the rest of her life—as the woman tricked by Justin Dupree. She might as well get used to it.

Though she wasn't going to forgive Cara and Kevin anytime soon. She'd eat dinner, be as cordial as she could manage, then go home and lock herself in her bedroom for the rest of the weekend. "Red, please."

"Great. It's a wonderful Malbec Kevin brought back from Argentina. And help yourself to my cheese puffs." Cara practically danced across the room.

Alicia moved slowly to a black leather chair. She wasn't sure she could eat a cheese puff without throwing up, let alone an entire dinner.

But if Justin expected her to turn and run, he was wrong.

"How was your week?" That soft, warm voice, with a touch of grit, crept over her.

"Fine, thanks." *No thanks to you.*

She scanned the room. Cara's inventive touch was visible in colorful accents and a bright, contemporary painting that lit up the wall.

She'd bet the whole place was black and white when Kevin lived here by himself. Cara shone a ray of bright light into everyone's life. It was a shame she'd never accept an invitation here again. She forced a smile as Cara handed her a glass.

"To new beginnings," said Cara gaily. When her toast was met with an awkward silence, her bright expression faltered. "Mine and Kevin's. We're happier than we've ever been."

"That's great." Alicia raised her glass. "I'm thrilled for you." Her words rang a little hollow, and the wine splashed in her glass as Justin moved closer to join the toast.

She shrank as his arm neared hers, though she let him clink his glass against hers. It was only polite, after all.

"Dinner will be ready in a couple of minutes. Let me go check on it." Cara hurried away to the kitchen, leaving Alicia in her chair with Kevin and Justin standing right over her.

"So, Justin, entering any yacht races this month?"

"The season's winding down but I might squeeze in one more if I'm in town the last week of the month. Depends on a few things."

Alicia could swear she felt Kevin glance down at her, but she kept her eyes firmly fixed on her glass.

"Alicia, have you ever been sailing?"

Kevin's question made her voice catch in her throat. She cleared it, but before she could speak, Justin cut in. "Alicia came out on my boat with me last week. She's a natural sailor."

"Did you enjoy it?" Kevin smiled at her expectantly.

Had Justin put him up to this? Her neck prickled with irritation.

"It was an interesting experience. I'm not sure I like drifting out in the middle of nowhere. I suspect I'm a landlubber at heart." She smiled pleasantly, though it felt more like a grimace.

"Nonsense! You took to the water like a mermaid." Justin's voice trickled into her ears again.

"A flattering comparison but I'm far more comfortable with feet than a fishtail."

She was damned if she'd meet his gaze. She stared at a point to the left of his head, so Kevin might think she was actually looking at him. There was no way she'd put herself at the mercy of those dangerous blue eyes and much-practiced charm.

"Some sports take a while to get used to," continued Kevin bravely. This little reunion must have been Justin's idea. Wasn't having her body at his mercy all weekend enough? "You really should give it another try."

"No, thanks." She sipped her wine and fixed a noncommittal smile on her face. "I think I'll stick to tennis."

"We should play doubles some time." Kevin leapt enthusiastically on her suggestion.

"That would be lovely," she said. "I'll tell Alex to dust off his racquet. He used to be on the school tennis team and I'm sure he'd love to play again."

Ha! Take that, conspirators.

"Dinner's ready!" called Cara from the kitchen. "Alicia, could you give me a hand with the dishes?"

"Sure," she said with relief. She excused herself and dove for the kitchen.

"Sorry," Cara said quietly. "It seemed like a good idea at the time."

"Justin set this up, didn't he?" whispered Alicia.

"I think it was actually Kevin's idea. Rather romantic. It's not often you get two guys putting their heads together to hatch a plan to hook a girl."

"Oh, I bet it's far more common that you'd imagine. Except that romance is not usually the aim." Alicia raised a brow.

"You're really not going to give him a chance, are you?"

"Nope. Would you like me to carry the salad?"

"Sure." Cara handed her a large majolica dish piled high with fresh vegetables. "People can change, you know."

"You mean, like Kevin?"

"Exactly. Men are slow to mature. Kind of like a fine wine."

"Or a baby elephant."

Cara laughed. "You're awful."

"Yeah, and I have every right to be." She pushed past Cara and out into the dining room. A wide doorway opened into the living room, and through it she glimpsed Kevin and Justin enjoying what looked like a casual conversation. How on earth was she going to survive an entire meal at the same table with that snake?

She deliberately sat next to him so that she wouldn't have to look at him. The table was large enough that she wasn't assaulted by his male scent, though it certainly was annoying having that low, seductive voice level with her ear.

Kevin brought out steaming bowls of fresh pasta, and Cara spooned spicy red sauce over them.

"How's the new exhibit coming along?" asked Justin, once they were settled.

Alicia stiffened. "Fine. We're unpacking the boxes on Monday."

"What's it about?" Kevin asked, pouring white wine for all of them.

"A traveling exhibition from the Smithsonian about changes in the environment."

"You mean, like global warming?" She felt Justin's bright gaze scorch the side of her face.

"Not really." She took childish pleasure in her negative answer. "Ancient changes. Oceans that became deserts, forests turned to stone, that kind of thing. We have some striking fossil samples to put on display, and three interactive video programs. I have school groups booked solid for the entire month."

"That's wonderful!" exclaimed Cara. "I know you've been trying hard to lure schools to the museum."

"Museums are about the living, not the dead," Alicia repeated her mantra. "And I'm thrilled, to be honest. It was a big deal getting the board to agree to host this exhibit and I'm hoping it's the start of a new era for the Somerset Museum of Natural History."

"I'm sure it will be. Here's to new beginnings!" Cara lifted her glass.

"I think you already said that, hon." Kevin leaned in and laid a kiss on her cheek. "But it's a nice thought, anyway."

"All right, I'll rephrase." Cara tossed her long blond curls. "Here's to new beginnings for things that got off to a lousy start in the first place."

Alicia pretended to sip her wine, but didn't. She was superstitious that way.

Besides, her relationship with Rick—*Justin*—got off to a fabulous start.

It was the part that came next which stank.

Kevin leaned in. "Justin, how was Hong Kong?"

"Busy, as usual. I had a lot of meetings but I didn't go out much. I couldn't wait to get back home." Again, his gaze warmed Alicia's cheek.

"I've slowed down on the traveling myself. Things that seem fun when you're right out of college definitely lose their luster as you gain maturity."

"Especially when you have a lovely woman to come home to." Justin's wistful tone almost crept under her skin.

Then it occurred to her she might not even be the woman he was talking about. She'd learned a few things about Justin Dupree since she'd found out the truth, and none of them was too flattering.

"How is Mila Jankovich?" The words shot out of her mouth.

How embarrassing that she even remembered the name from the social pages. Unfortunately, it was burned on her brain in flaming scarlet letters.

A stunned silence followed her question. Now it was really awkward that she didn't turn and look at Justin, since everyone was staring at her. She speared a broccoli floret and lifted it to her lips, though her stomach had contracted shut.

"I don't know." Justin spoke softly. "I haven't seen her in a while. I think she still lives in New York."

"Alicia and I saw a picture of you with her in *Vanity Fair*," explained Cara. "Is it true that she barely speaks English?"

"Her English isn't bad. She has a funny Canadian accent because she learned from an exchange student who came to live with her in the Ukraine. She's actually a lot nicer than she looks when she's not giving that supermodel stare for one camera or another, but she and I were never more than casual companions."

"So you never dated?" asked Cara, like a journalist who reasks a question that's just been answered. Alicia knew what her friend was doing on her behalf, but mostly still she wished she'd never mentioned Mila's name.

"I took her to a couple of social events. A friend of mine runs her agency and he wanted her to be seen with the 'right people.'" He chuckled. "Kind of scary that I'm the right people, but I didn't mind since they were charity events I'd have gone to anyway." He paused and

Alicia felt her skin burn again. "There's someone else I'd much rather have taken."

The awkward pause stretched on for a full thirty seconds, while Alicia forked individual peas from the inside of a mange-tout. She was done being a sucker for Justin Dupree's notorious charms.

"Great puttanesca sauce, sweetheart." Kevin kissed Cara on the neck and she blushed.

"It's delicious," chimed Alicia, glad the conversation had turned neutral again.

"Thanks. I've never made it before. I wasn't sure about the capers but I think they really add a zing to it."

"It's perfect," said Justin. "Best food I've eaten all week."

"I'll go start getting dessert ready." Cara rose from her seat with obvious enthusiasm. Alicia was about to run after her to offer help, but Kevin was quicker. He tracked her out of the room like a shadow.

"Alicia…" His deep, seductive voice made Alicia's back stiffen.

"Yes, *Justin?*" She picked up her water and took a sip. She didn't dare drink any more wine in case she became susceptible.

"Don't you think this is a little silly?"

"Me sipping my water?"

"You refusing to look at me." If she wasn't mistaken, she heard an edge of unease in his voice, different from his usual confident banter.

"Don't flatter yourself. I'm not refusing to look at you. I just have better things to look at."

She cast about the table for something to fix her eyes on. The cut-glass carafe filled with salad dressing worked.

"Are you *afraid* to look at me?"

"Afraid? Why on earth would I be afraid?"

"It just seems odd that you won't meet my eye. I'd think you'd at least want to give me a stony glare or something."

"Why, would that be exciting for you?" She twirled her wineglass between her fingers. "I think you've had enough fun at my expense, don't you?"

She rose from her chair and headed for the windows. The penthouse apartment had wide French doors that opened onto a balcony with a view over Houston. She tried the stainless steel handle and it opened easily.

Phew. Alicia stepped outside and inhaled the cool evening air.

The setting sun glistened on thousands of glass windows, making the city glitter like a mosaic. No doubt other people down there, in all those cars and houses and apartments, were suffering. Her petty concerns were nothing compared to some of the real problems people had.

All she wanted to do was forget about Justin and get on with her life. Which had been perfectly fine before she met him, thank you very much.

"Alicia." His voice came from the doorway behind her.

"That's my name. At least we're in agreement on that."

"I'm so terribly sorry about what happened." His voice was gruff with emotion.

Alicia's breath caught in her lungs. Something told her not to blurt out a snappy comeback.

"If I could turn back the clock to our first meeting and introduce myself as Justin Dupree, I'd do it in a heartbeat."

"Except that then my friends would have warned me against you." She tilted her head to the evening breeze, trying to cool her flushed face. "I'd never have gone to stay the night with a notorious womanizer."

"I know. That's one of the many reasons why…why I love you."

The words took a split second to sink in. Then Alicia's brain spat them out. He didn't love her. He just couldn't stand not to have someone eating out of his palm. He wanted to charm her and get her back on his good side, so he wouldn't have any embarrassing unfinished business with her.

She fixed her gaze on the distant purple horizon.

"I do, you know." He moved closer. "Love you."

Her heart squeezed. "You don't. You barely know me."

"I know you enough to see that you are a rare and amazing woman."

"Well, I'm not." Her voice shook slightly. "You only want me now that I'm not available, so you've painted a fantastical picture of me in your head. I'm a quiet, rather dull museum curator, with—as you know only too well—almost no experience with the opposite sex." She sniffed. "I'd hardly call that amazing. And there's nothing rare about me."

"Trust me, there is." His voice drew closer. "You are the only—and I mean *the only*—woman who's been horrified to find out that I'm actually Justin Dupree. I started using a fake name because when I introduced myself as Justin Dupree, women would start pawing me and hanging on my every word like I was Einstein. When I was a kid I enjoyed female attention, but after a while, I got pretty tired of wondering whether a woman was genuinely interested in *me* or if she just liked my family name and all the millions that came with it."

"What a cross to bear."

"I know." He laughed. "It does sound ridiculous. Not many people have the luxury of complaining that they have too much money and too many women fawning over them."

His body heat radiated through her clothes as he moved closer. "But it hurts when people don't see you. When all they see is the name and the money and everything that can do for them. And if you're surrounded by people like that, your life starts feeling pretty empty, no matter how busy you are."

Her skin prickled at his nearness. Any minute now, she expected him to slide his arms around her waist in the proprietary manner that only a few days ago she'd found so charming.

But he didn't.

"You're not like that, Alicia." He hesitated, and she could almost feel his breath on her cheek. "You're not at all impressed by money or power or the trappings of prestige. You judge everything according to your own exacting standards. I realized that pretty fast and I knew I'd made a mistake in giving you a false name. I planned to tell you the truth, but then the fire happened and I didn't want to upset you when you had plenty to be upset about already."

Alicia wanted to snark, *How thoughtful.* But the words stayed on her tongue. It was thoughtful. He could easily have blurted out the truth. What did he have to lose?

Her in his bed?

He hadn't actually tried to get her into bed at all. He'd kissed her good-night and hustled away to his own bedroom. She was the one who dragged him into bed.

"I love you, Alicia." His soft voice crept over her like light from the last rays of the sun.

His words were so…heartfelt. They bypassed her anger and humiliation and touched something inside her.

"I know we haven't spent very much time together, but I've lived long enough to know something good when I see it. And what we have is very, very good. I can talk to you about anything. You're curious and enthusiastic. You truly appreciate the world around us, and the people in it." He paused, and drew in a deep breath. "You bring magic into every day and I'd like to spend the rest of my life with you."

Alicia's heart nearly stopped. *What did he just say?*

Adrenaline flashed through her, making her hands twitch. She couldn't possibly ignore him anymore. Even if it was just an act, he'd gone too far.

She turned, slowly, to face him. She found his handsome face taut with emotion. His deep blue eyes shone with passion and—as she knew it would—his imploring gaze sent a ray of tenderness right to her heart.

His arms hung by his sides, but she could see from the

set of his shoulders that he itched to wrap them around her. "When I was in Hong Kong, I couldn't think of anything but coming home to you." He looked into her eyes. "All the things I used to like—going out to clubs, hanging out with friends, even taking a boat out on the water—nothing seemed fun without you there to share it."

Alicia blinked. Something like hope bloomed in her chest. She was starting to truly believe him.

Then common sense splashed her brain like cold water. "But we've only been on a few dates. Maybe you're just…attracted to me." She didn't dare believe it was more.

Though she had to admit that she'd been all but convinced he was "the one" before she found out about his name.

He tilted his head and a wry expression appeared on his face. "I know what attraction feels like. My reputation as a ladies' man is no secret, and I admit there's some fire behind that smoke. But what I feel for you is very different. It confused me, to be honest. I've always avoided emotional commitments. I never wanted a serious relationship." His blue gaze darkened and the force of it threatened to knock her off her high heels. "But with you, I want so much that I don't even know where it ends. I don't want it to end, ever."

She felt his hands at her waist—tentative at first, then firmer as her body yielded instantly to his touch. A deep sigh escaped her as she melted into his arms and their lips met. The kiss exploded through her, sending energy all the way to her fingers and toes.

Oh, Justin. His real name filled her mind, with the

knowledge that he really was still the sweet, fun, exciting and caring man she'd spent that blissful weekend with.

The name was different but nothing else had changed.

She held him close, her fingers pressing into the muscle of his back and her head angled to his kiss. Justin's arms wrapped around her and crushed her to his hard chest.

She'd tried so hard to push all thoughts of him from her mind, to forget all the dreams and hopes she'd enjoyed and reimagine her future without him in it. Now, in his arms, all the joy and anticipation and excitement came flooding back.

And the desire. Her nipples tightened against his firm muscle and heat flooded her belly. Her body throbbed with arousal and her fingers itched with a sudden urge to unbutton his crisp pale blue shirt and tug it off.

But they were outside on a balcony, illuminated by the glow of the setting sun.

"Justin," she breathed, tugging her lips from his with considerable effort.

A smile lifted his mouth and lit his eyes. "You used my real name."

"You're still…you."

"I certainly hope so." His perplexed expression almost made her laugh.

He was the same man she'd fallen in love with. And yes, it was love. Otherwise it wouldn't have hurt so badly when she tried to tell herself it was over.

"Rick Jones, Justin Dupree—they're just names." She bit her lip. "Maybe I made too much of the difference."

"I never intended to deceive you. I just wanted to meet you as…a man. Not as someone with a price tag and a list of expectations attached."

"Well, Justin Dupree, I guess it's nice to finally meet you." She reached out and pushed his hair back off his forehead. "You're pretty cute, you know?"

"Thanks." His adorable, dimpled smile weakened her knees a little further. "You're not half-bad yourself. But it wasn't your gorgeous face or your breathtaking body that I missed."

"No?" She lifted a brow.

"Nope." He shrugged. "I missed talking with you. I missed your smile, and the way your eyes sparkle when you're excited. I missed your laugh, and the way you sigh when something moves you."

Alicia swallowed hard. His emotion showed in his voice, and in the lines of his handsome face. Oh, boy. She was falling for him all over again. And how could she not?

She put her hands on her hips. "You didn't miss my body at all?"

Justin cocked his head. "Okay, maybe I missed it a bit."

"You didn't miss my kisses?" She narrowed her eyes.

He looked sheepish. "I'd be lying if I said I didn't."

"And you're never going to lie to me again, are you?" She leveled a hard stare right at those baby blues.

"Never." He said it slowly, enunciating each syllable. "On my life, I will never lie to you again."

Tears welled in her eyes, but she tried to blink them back. "I lied, too, so I could be with you." She wiped away a tear that spilled out. "So, I know how it happens. I lied to my brother, who I love more than anyone."

Except maybe you.

"Did you ever tell him you came to stay with me, instead?"

"I did. He was mad, but he got over it. I think he knows he was trying too hard to protect me, and it backfired."

"And I was trying too hard to make you like me, and that backfired, too."

Alicia inhaled a shaky breath. "I do like you, Justin Dupree." She blinked and he reached out to wipe away her tear. "I like you very much."

His smile threatened to break into a grin.

Joy swelled inside her. "I think I might even be able to look past all that embarrassing wealth and notoriety you're saddled with."

"That's big of you." His grin broadened. "Not many people could be so open-minded."

"I even like your name—Justin—it has a nice ring to it."

"Justin and Alicia. It's a stylish combination, don't you think?" His gaze sparkled with warmth.

Alicia nodded, emotion flooding her chest. A sudden image of the letters *J & A* etched on a wineglass, or embroidered in linen napkins, snuck into her brain.

Get a hold of yourself, she thought.

But she really didn't want to. Right now she wanted to let go. To shed all the doubt and fear and insecurity that had plagued her, and revel in the sweet joy of this perfect moment.

Except that they were on a balcony. At someone else's apartment.

"We really should go back inside. Cara and Kevin are probably wondering what happened to us."

Justin laughed. "They might think you pushed me off."

"I'm still pretty mad at you." She pursed her lips. "But I think I can get over it. I know from my brother's experience that sometimes life can be a pain in the butt when everyone has an opinion about you before they meet you."

He nodded. "It's annoying when people start out with a cartoon version of you in their heads, and you have to work to show them there's a real person in there, too."

"Yeah. Poor Alex." She grinned. "And poor you, too." She pressed a kiss to his lips, which sent a ripple of desire shivering to her toes.

"Would you have dated me if you knew I was Justin Dupree?"

"No way." She shook her head. "I've got a reputation to protect."

"You'd have known your carefully guarded virginity was in mortal danger."

"True." She pretended to look thoughtful. "So in fact, maybe I would have chased after you myself. And then you'd have wondered if I just wanted you for your money and your fancy name."

"I'm not sure I would have cared, in your case." He kissed her. "I'd have just counted myself lucky."

Alicia leaned her head against his chest, enjoying his natural male scent and the steadiness of his strong body. "We do have something really good together."

She glanced up, taking in the strength of his chin and his chiseled cheek. "Whoever you are."

His chuckle shook them both. "I'm glad you're not holding my double identity against me anymore."

"Guess it proves you can get used to anything. Though if I call out 'Rick!' while we're making love, you have no one to blame but yourself," she teased.

He growled and nipped at her cheek. "If you're calling out while we're making love, it's all good as far as I'm concerned." He tightened his arms around her. "I missed you so much."

"I missed you, too," she confessed. "I tried like heck not to. That's why I was so mad at you. I couldn't get you out of my mind."

"That's because we're meant to be together." His fingers caressed her back, heating her skin through her thin dress. "Alicia, I want to ask you something, and you don't have to give your reply right away. You can think about it for a day, a week, a month, as long as you want. I have to ask though, or I'm going to explode."

She swallowed. "Sure." Fear zinged in her stomach. "Go ahead." What could he ask after such a preamble? Her heart beat in terror and anticipation.

He pulled back a fraction, so she could look up into his face.

The last bronze rays of light illuminated his features, and emotion darkened his gaze. "Alicia Montoya, I love you and I want to spend the rest of my life with you. Will you marry me?"

Ten

Justin held his breath. He didn't think she'd say yes, but for some crazy reason he had to ask anyway.

Patience had never been a virtue he could brag about.

And he wanted Alicia to know that she wasn't just another woman to him, but the woman he wanted to spend the rest of his life with.

Alicia's big brown eyes filled with tears. "I love you, too, Justin." She said his name deliberately, but with warmth, as if she accepted his name and the real him that came with it.

She blinked, teardrops glittering on her long, dark lashes. "I know you don't need an answer right away, and that the sensible thing to do would be to wait. We could date for a while, get to know each other. But—" She inhaled sharply. "I've never met anyone like you. Not because you're rich and influential and all that other stuff, but because you're thoughtful and caring and you really appreciate the opportunities life offers you, and you live each day to the fullest." She swallowed and blinked again. "And I would like to marry you."

"Yes!" Justin lifted her up in the air and she shrieked. Her body felt featherlight in his arms as he spun her around. Joy and excitement surged through him and he kissed her with force. "We'll have a fantastic life together."

"Are you psychic?" she asked, laughing.

"No, just smart." He grinned. "And so are you, so you know I'm right."

"You're not very modest though, are you?"

"Not at all." He shrugged. "Sorry."

Alicia narrowed her eyes. "There is one thing you must do, before we can marry."

Uh-oh. The serious look on her face sent a shard of alarm to his gut. "What?"

"You must ask my brother for permission." Mischief sparkled in her stern gaze.

"What if he doesn't give it?" Justin cocked his head.

"You have to convince him to give it." A naughty smile crept across her sensual mouth. "Old-school style."

"Oh, boy." Justin frowned. "So, I have to promise to give him a herd of cattle for your hand in marriage or something?"

She winced. "It better be a good herd, with some prize bulls. And make sure you tell him he has to give me away at the wedding."

"Hmm." He chewed his lip. "I might need to add some wagons loaded with gold bullion."

"I'm sure you'll think of something." She grinned. "You're good at talking people around."

"I'm certainly glad I managed with you." He stroked her back, enjoying her softness through her delicate dress. "I didn't want to spend the rest of my life missing you and being miserable. Kevin told me how lost he felt without Cara all those years."

Alicia gasped. "We'd better go back in."

They unwove their arms from around each other. Alicia straightened Justin's shirt collar and he removed a smudge of mascara from under her eye with his thumb.

He took her hand and stepped back through the French doors. No sign of the apartment's owners. The door to the kitchen still closed and no dessert on the table.

"Kevin? Cara?" Alicia walked past him. "We're back and we have some news."

Cara and Kevin came out of the kitchen. "We were wondering what you two were up to," said Cara. "We wanted to give you some privacy."

Alicia tucked her hair behind her ears. "We went out on the balcony."

"Well, I'm glad no one got pushed off." She glanced from one to the other.

"We made up," said Alicia with a shy smile. "In fact, we more than made up."

"We're getting married," said Justin, unable to keep a proud grin from spreading across his face.

Cara let out a shriek and tore across the room to Alicia. She kissed her hard on both cheeks. "That's wonderful!" She grabbed Justin and kissed him, too. "I'm thrilled for you both!"

Kevin beamed. "I don't think Cara was ever going to forgive herself if you two didn't get back together. She's done nothing but mutter about how she should have kept her damn mouth shut. So, you've made my wife happy as well as your future bride."

"She'll be my bride as soon as I can convince her brother to give her away."

"Oh, boy." Kevin grimaced. "Better wear a bullet-proof vest when you go ask."

"Alex isn't that bad," protested Alicia. "He's just a little overprotective."

"He's a lot overprotective." Cara grinned. "I wish I could be a fly on the wall at that meeting."

Justin's steady nerves were a point of pride, so he didn't at all like the way his finger shook slightly as he pressed the buzzer at the gates of El Diablo.

He'd called to set up a meeting with Alex, but his messages had gone unanswered. Alicia had simply shrugged and told him Alex wasn't great at returning calls, so he should stop by the ranch.

He could swear she had a gleam in her eye at the time. She wanted him to prove his love for her.

Well, damn it, he would.

The intercom crackled to life and a voice grunted, "Yeah?"

Alex. Apparently, he took personal charge of the security system.

"Alex, Justin Dupree here." He went for authoritative confidence. "I'd like to talk to you about Alicia."

To his surprise, the iron gates started to swing open.

So far, so good. Justin piloted his Porsche inside. The

hair on the back of his neck prickled a bit when he glanced in the rearview mirror and saw the gates swing closed behind him.

Calm down. He's your future brother-in-law. If this Brody thing ever gets settled, you might even be friends one day.

He wondered if Alicia was home. Perhaps she was watching secretly from one of the windows.

She'd refused to move in with him until they were formally engaged, so he was pretty sure he wouldn't see her in his bed again until he got Alex on his side.

The big barn was being rebuilt and the sidewalls were already framed. A tall figure strode out from the construction site, sleeves rolled up over powerful forearms and a grim expression on his hard-edged face.

Justin pulled the car to the side of the drive and climbed out. "Alex, good to see you."

"I wish I could say the same. Still, we're shorthanded here raising the roof. Come this way."

Justin's eyes widened as Alex disappeared back into the wood skeleton of the barn.

Anything it takes, baby, I promise. Whatever Alex made him do, Alicia was worth it.

With his next breath, he followed him in.

"Got a greenhorn here," bellowed Alex. "But he's light so he can climb up to the rafters."

Justin swallowed as he glanced up to the high sill where the roof would rest. He could see the trusses stacked at the far end of the barn frame, with a crane ready to hoist them into place.

"Whatever you say, boss," said an older man at the controls of the crane.

"Wear this." Alex flung a scuffed yellow hard hat at Justin, and he caught it and put it on. "There's a ladder up at this end where the first truss will be raised. You steady on your feet?"

"Sure am."

Alex's stern face betrayed no emotion as he tossed Justin a pair of worn leather gloves and a spirit level. But he could swear he saw a twinkle of evil in his eye.

Justin scaled the tall aluminum ladder leaning against the frame. He'd climbed masts higher than this out on a heaving ocean. Still, he hadn't had a man who hated him at the tiller that time.

At the top of the ladder, he stepped up onto the sill. "What's the plan?"

He saw the first triangular truss rise off the ground, lifted by the crane. It swung slowly toward him. Three other men climbed up into position around him.

"They'll get the ends," said Alex. "You line up the middle of the truss with the sill and check it for plumb. When it's right, Joe will nail it down."

Great. As long as the truss didn't knock him to the ground, he might survive to enjoy marriage to Alicia.

He steadied himself on the sill, which happily was almost a foot wide.

Alex must know about his plans with Alicia. If he didn't he wouldn't have let him in here. This was a test. If he passed, he'd be home free.

Or at least that was a good thought to keep in mind as the heavy truss floated through the air toward him. As it moved within reach, Justin grabbed the truss and helped settle it in position at his feet, while the guys at both ends did the same.

He checked it for level. "It's dead on."

Pneumatic nailers fixed it into position with loud thunking sounds. "One down, twenty-nine more to go." Alex looked up with a grin. "Though for the next one, you'll have to move out along the center beam."

Justin looked down at his feet where a long span stretched to the next support column. He lifted his head high.

"No problem."

Alicia was worth it.

He wasn't surprised to see her standing nearby when he finally climbed down from the barn frame nearly five hours later. They'd raised thirty trusses to form the biggest roof he'd ever seen in his life.

She came across the lawn toward him. "Great job, guys! Come on in the house and have something to eat."

Justin glanced down. His light blue shirt was drenched with sweat and a layer of fine sawdust coated his entire body. Alicia clearly didn't mind though. Her big dark eyes sparkled with...triumph?

Apparently, he'd done something right.

"The barn looks fantastic. It's going to be nice to have all that extra space for the calves."

"You're right, 'Manita. I know you were sad about the old barn burning, but this one will be a lot more useful."

"I'm glad Justin was able to help."

He caught sight of her grin before she turned back to the house.

Inside, he found the kitchen table piled high with freshly made tortilla fixings. Alicia snapped the lids off two cold beers and set them down.

"Come help yourselves." She handed them each a plate. "I have to run down to the post office before it closes. Eat up, and I'll be back in a few." She gave Justin a knowing look as she marched past him. *Now's your chance,* the look seemed to say.

"Help yourself. You earned a good meal," grunted Alex. "You're stronger than you look."

"I enjoyed it." He wasn't entirely lying. "I never did any construction before. It's eye-opening to see how things go together."

"A well-constructed building can last a thousand years. Even a wood building, as long as it doesn't burn down."

A brief silence settled in the room as they loaded rice and chicken onto warm tortillas.

Justin glanced up. "Are the police any closer to finding out who set the fire?"

"You don't think I did it?" Alex lifted a dark brow. "That seems to be the word around town."

"People are scared of what they don't understand. They start flinging accusations about."

"People like your friends Mitch and Lance Brody?"

"I think you all know that none of you are involved in any of this." Justin spooned some guacamole on to his plate.

"Lance Brody outright accused me. Darius told me he was going around telling people someone saw my truck at the scene."

"I'm sure the fire upset him and he started grasping at straws. I told him myself I was sure you didn't have anything to do with it."

Alex stared at him for a long moment. "You did?"

"Sure. The way Alicia talked about you, I knew you'd never be involved in something like that."

"Alicia talked about me?" Alex's grim expression softened into surprise.

"She talks about you a lot. She really looks up to you."

"Huh." His grunt contained more emotion than he probably intended to reveal.

"The problem is, if you didn't set the Brody fire, and the Brodys didn't set your fire, then who's wandering around Somerset carrying chemical accelerants'?"

"And why?" Alex frowned.

"Someone who has a bone to pick with both you and the Brodys."

Alex snorted. "What in the heck do I have in common with the Brody brothers that would make someone come after both of us?"

Justin picked up a fork from a pile of gleaming cutlery. "Well, one thing occurs to me. You're all fairly new members of the Texas Cattleman's Club."

"What does that have to do with anything?"

"Honestly, I have no idea." Justin shrugged. "But something strange is going on—the fires, the money missing from the club's accounts—and I have a feeling it's all connected somehow."

"Do the Brody brothers still have me at the top of their list of suspects?"

"I doubt it, but I confess I haven't seen 'em in a while. There's only one person I want to spend my free time with these days." Justin spooned sour cream onto his tortilla.

"I suspected as much." Alex picked up his beer and headed for the door. "Let's sit out back."

"Out back" was a wide, shady veranda with potted daisies and an expansive view of the back forty. Or the back four hundred, which is what it looked like. Sturdy cattle grazed as far as the eye could see.

Alex eased himself into a wooden chair, and Justin took the bench beside him.

"I love your sister." There, he'd said it. "We got off on the wrong foot, but she knows I care about her and she's prepared to forgive me and look to the future." Justin inhaled the cool evening air. "I'm hoping you're willing to do the same."

"That's a lot to hope for." Alex took a hearty bite of his rolled tortilla.

"I've asked her to marry me, and she said yes, but only on the condition that you'll give her away."

Alex stopped chewing. "You asked her to *marry* you?" He stared. "You only just met."

So she hadn't told Alex. She'd trusted him to sort things out on his own. Her faith in him warmed his heart still further.

"It doesn't take a lot of time to know you've met the right person."

His dark eyes narrowed. "You gave her a ring?"

"Not yet. I wanted to get your permission first. Alicia's old-fashioned." He couldn't help smiling. "That's one of the many things I love about her."

Alex still looked as if someone had smacked him with a two-by-four. "You actually proposed marriage? And here I thought you were just hoping to take her out on a date again."

"Alicia and I want to be together. We're both adults. Why waste time?"

"You caught me off guard." Alex blew out a long breath. "I was pretty impressed you were prepared to frame a barn just to win a date with her."

"I'd frame a barn for the chance to see her smile."

"I'm beginning to believe you would." Alex frowned. "Our parents got married after only one evening together. They just knew." He shook his head. "I guess it works that way sometimes."

"I didn't think I'd ever fall in love, but then I'd never met someone like Alicia."

Alex put down his plate. "Alicia's used to a certain lifestyle." He leaned forward. "I've worked hard to provide it for her."

"I can guarantee she'll have everything she wants. I own a good-size shipping company and we—"

"I know, I know." Alex's frown deepened and he stared off into the distance. "Damn, I hate the idea of losing Alicia to another man." He turned to Justin "That sounds bad, and I don't mean it like that, but she's my baby sister." He picked up his plate again and took a giant bite of his tortilla.

Justin did the same, and they chewed in silence for a moment. Then he took a deep steady breath. "Will you give Alicia away at our wedding?"

Alex looked up at the horizon. The sky had turned mauve and cast an eerie glow over the fields of cattle. "I know you've got a lot of money, but Alicia needs more than that." He fixed his gaze on Justin. "She's tough on the outside but soft and gentle inside. If you break her heart I'll…" The look in his eyes said it all.

"I'll cherish her and treat her with respect and love. I promise you that." Justin swallowed.

Hope surged in his chest as he saw Alex's expression soften.

"Then I give you my blessing." He turned to Justin. His stern features showed some of the pain he'd no doubt experience at losing Alicia from his daily existence. "And yes, I'll give her away. But if you don't treat her right, you can count on it that I'll come take her back." Alex glared for a second, striking alarm into Justin's heart. But then he simply said, "Congratulations, brother-in-law."

Justin's chest ached with joy. "I appreciate your trust. I promise you I'll earn it every day."

Justin extended his hand and Alex shook it with a quick nod. "I believe you will," Alex said.

"You'd better both go have a shower and clean up," said Alicia, as she stepped through the French doors out on to the patio, looking radiant as a sunrise. "Because we're all going out to celebrate."

"Were you listening the whole time?" Alex cocked his head.

"No, I really did go to the post office. But I heard the important parts."

Her shy smile made Justin's heart leap.

Then she turned to Alex and took his hands in hers. "And I'm very glad you're going to give me away at my wedding. You've always been the most important man in my life, and everything I am today, I owe to you."

Justin watched her brawny older brother tear up.

Alex pressed a kiss to Alicia's forehead. "You're the best sister a brother could hope for and I wish you all the happiness in the world. The two of you are welcome to live at El Diablo, by the way. I don't like the idea of my baby sister living in sin at a hotel."

"Alex! It's the twenty-first century. They don't call it living in sin anymore."

"I call a spade a spade. Even if you are getting married."

"If I listened to you, I wouldn't be getting married. I'd have gone to stay with that sleazy El Gato." She did a mock shiver. "Luckily, I decided to trust my own instincts for once."

She smiled at Justin. "I'd be happy to live with you wherever you are."

"As long as there's a ring on your finger," growled Alex.

"Speaking of which…" Justin reached into the back pocket of his pants and pulled out a small ring box. He turned to face Alicia, then lowered himself slowly to one knee. He wanted to do it the old-fashioned way—even in front of her brother—because he knew she'd like that.

"Alicia Montoya, will you be my wife?"

"Oh, Justin." Her hands flew to her mouth as tears glazed her eyes. "How thoughtful!" Her voice wavered. "And yes, I will be your wife."

He flipped open the small, white velvet box. Inside shone the most spectacular diamond he'd been able to find in the entire Houston area. It was nearly four carats and glittered like the Gulf of Mexico.

"Oh, my goodness." Alicia's eyes widened.

Justin pulled the ring from its satin bed and slid it onto her finger.

"Oh, Justin, it's so beautiful!" Alicia admired the sparkly gem on her finger.

"I had it set in platinum since I notice you prefer silver jewelry."

"It's perfect." She looked up at him, eyes shining with tears. "You're perfect."

"Oh, I'm a long way from perfect, but with you by my side I'll be the best I can be." He grinned, almost delirious with happiness. He turned to Alex. "And I have no intention of keeping Alicia prisoner in a high-rise hotel. I think we should buy a house in Somerset—perhaps one with a tennis court, since I know Alicia likes tennis."

"And a pool," said Alex with a serious expression. "She likes to swim and it gets hot in the summer."

"What about a lake?" Alicia's eyes sparkled with humor. "For you to sail on?"

Justin laughed and had to stop himself from pulling her into his arms.

"I think a sweet little house with a nice little garden would be just fine," she said. "And the sooner we get married, the less time I'll be living in sin."

She tilted her head and looked up at Justin. "Could we get married here at El Diablo? That would mean a lot to me. If it's okay with Alex."

"Of course," both men replied instantly. They glanced at each other and a half-smile formed on Alex's face.

"I can tell we're going to be a very happy family," said Alicia with a smile. She looked at Justin shyly. "And maybe our new house can have some extra bedrooms, in case our family gets bigger."

Justin's chest swelled almost to bursting. "I can't wait."

"Then you guys better shower and change so we can go celebrate our engagement."

"Great idea," said Justin. "Where shall we go?"

Alicia smiled and admired her ring. "Why, the Texas Cattleman's Club of course. Where else?"

* * * * *

Don't miss the last book in our
TEXAS CATTLEMAN'S CLUB *series,*
LONE STAR SEDUCTION,
available next month from Silhouette Desire.
You won't want to miss it!

*Celebrate 60 years of pure reading
pleasure with Harlequin®!
Just in time for the holidays,
Silhouette Special Edition® is proud
to present* New York Times *bestselling
author Kathleen Eagle's*
ONE COWBOY, ONE CHRISTMAS

Rodeo rider Zach Beaudry was a travelin' man—
until he broke down in middle-of-nowhere South
Dakota during a deep freeze. That's when an
angel came to his rescue....

"Don't die on me. Come on, Zel. You know how much I love you, girl. You're all I've got. Don't do this to me here. Not *now*."

But Zelda had quit on him, and Zach Beaudry had no one to blame but himself. He'd taken his sweet time hitting the road, and then miscalculated a shortcut. For all he knew he was a hundred miles from gas. But even if they were sitting next to a pump, the ten dollars he had in his pocket wouldn't get him out of South Dakota, which was not where he wanted to be right now. Not even his beloved pickup truck, Zelda, could get him much of anywhere on fumes. He was sitting out in the cold in the middle of nowhere. And getting colder.

He shifted the pickup into Neutral and pulled hard on the steering wheel, using the downhill slope to get her off the blacktop and into the roadside grass, where she shuddered to a standstill. He stroked the padded dash. "You'll be safe here."

But Zach would not. It was getting dark, and it was already too damn cold for his cowboy ass. Zach's battered body was a barometer, and he was feeling South Dakota, big-time. He'd have given his right arm to be climbing into a hotel hot tub instead of a brutal blast of north wind. The right was his free arm anyway. Damn thing had lost altitude, touched some part of the bull and caused him a scoreless ride last time out.

It wasn't scoring him a ride this night, either. A carload of teenagers whizzed by, topping off the insult by laying on the horn as they passed him. It was at least twenty minutes before another vehicle came along. He stepped out and waved both arms this time, damn near getting himself killed. Whatever happened to *do unto others?* In places like this, decent people didn't leave each other stranded in the cold.

His face was feeling stiff, and he figured he'd better start walking before his toes went numb. He struck out for a distant yard light, the only sign of human habitation in sight. He couldn't tell how distant, but he knew he'd be hurting by the time he got there, and he was counting on some kindly old man to be answering the door. No shame among the lame.

It wasn't like Zach was fresh off the operating table—it had been a few months since his last round of repairs—but he hadn't given himself enough time. He'd lopped a couple of weeks off the near end of the doc's estimated recovery time, rigged up a brace, done some heavy-duty taping and climbed onto another bull. Hung in there for five seconds—four seconds past feeling the pop in his hip and three seconds short of the buzzer.

He could still feel the pain shooting down his leg with every step. Only this time he had to pick the damn thing up, swing it forward and drop it down again on his own.

Pride be damned, he just hoped *somebody* would be answering the door at the end of the road. The light in the front window was a good sign.

The four steps to the covered porch might as well have been four hundred, and he was looking to climb them with a lead weight chained to his left leg. His eyes were just as screwed up as his hip. Big black spots danced around with tiny red flashers, and he couldn't tell what was real and what wasn't. He stumbled over some shrubbery, steadied himself on the porch railing and peered between vertical slats.

There in the front window stood a spruce tree with a silver star affixed to the top. Zach was pretty sure the red sparks were all in his head, but the white lights twinkling by the hundreds throughout the huge tree, those were real. He wasn't too sure about the woman hanging the shiny balls. Most of her hair was caught up on her head and fastened in a curly clump, but the light captured by the escaped bits crowned her with a golden halo. Her face was a soft shadow, her body a willowy silhouette beneath a long white gown. If this was where the mind ran off to when cold started shutting down the rest of the body, then Zach's final worldly thought was, *This ain't such a bad way to go.*

If she would just turn to the window, he could die looking into the eyes of a Christmas angel.

* * * * *

Could this woman from Zach's past
get the lonesome cowboy to come in
from the cold…for good?
Look for
ONE COWBOY, ONE CHRISTMAS
by Kathleen Eagle
Available December 2009
from Silhouette Special Edition®

HARLEQUIN
Ambassadors

Want to share your passion for reading Harlequin® Books?

Become a Harlequin Ambassador!

Harlequin Ambassadors are a group of passionate and well-connected readers who are willing to share their joy of reading Harlequin® books with family and friends.

You'll be sent all the tools you need to spark great conversation, including free books!

All we ask is that you share the romance with your friends and family!

You'll also be invited to have a say in new book ideas and exchange opinions with women just like you!

To see if you qualify* to be a Harlequin Ambassador, please visit www.HarlequinAmbassadors.com.

*Please note that not everyone who applies to be a Harlequin Ambassador will qualify. For more information please visit www.HarlequinAmbassadors.com.

Thank you for your participation.

BAP09BPA

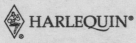

HARLEQUIN®

A Cowboy Christmas
MARIN THOMAS

2 stories in 1!

The holidays are a rough time for widower
Logan Taylor and single dad Fletcher McFadden—
neither hunky cowboy has been lucky in love.
But Christmas is the season of miracles! Logan
meets his match in "A Christmas Baby," while
Fletcher gets a second chance at love in "Marry
Me, Cowboy." This year both cowboys are on
Santa's Nice list!

Available December
wherever books are sold.

"LOVE, HOME & HAPPINESS"

www.eHarlequin.com

HAR75292

REQUEST YOUR FREE BOOKS!

2 FREE NOVELS PLUS 2 FREE GIFTS!

Silhouette *Desire*®

Passionate, Powerful, Provocative!

SDES09R

Silhouette Desire

COMING NEXT MONTH
Available December 8, 2009

#1981 HIGH-POWERED, HOT-BLOODED—Susan Mallery
Man of the Month
Crowned the country's meanest CEO, he needs a public overhaul.
His solution: a sweet-natured kindergarten teacher who will turn
him into an angel...though he's having a devil of a time keeping
his hands off her!

#1982 THE MAVERICK—Diana Palmer
Long, Tall Texans
Cowboy Harley Fowler is in the midst of mayhem—is seduction
the answer? Don't miss this story of a beloved hero readers have
been waiting to see fall in love!

#1983 LONE STAR SEDUCTION—Day Leclaire
Texas Cattleman's Club: Maverick County Millionaires
He finally has everything he's always wanted within his grasp.
He just can't allow himself to fall for the one woman who nearly
destroyed his empire...no matter how much he still wants her.

#1984 TO TAME HER TYCOON LOVER—Ann Major
Foolishly she'd given her innocence to the rich boy next door...
only to have her heart broken. Years later, she's vowed not to fall
for his seductive ways again. But she'd forgotten the tycoon's
undeniable magnetism and pure determination.

#1985 MILLIONAIRE UNDER THE MISTLETOE—
Tessa Radley
After unexpectedly sleeping with her family's secret benefactor,
she's taken by surprise when he proposes a more permanent
arrangement—as his wife!

#1986 DEFIANT MISTRESS, RUTHLESS MILLIONAIRE—
Yvonne Lindsay
Bent on ruining his father's company, he lures his new assistant
away from the man. But the one thing he never expects is a
double-cross! Will she stick to her mission or fall victim to her
new boss's seduction?

SDCNMBPA1109